The Library of Scandinavian Literature

IN SEARCH OF MY BELOVED

IN SEARCH *OF MY* BELOVED

THORBERGUR THORDARSON

TRANSLATED FROM THE ICELANDIC BY
KENNETH G. CHAPMAN

INTRODUCTION BY
KRISTJÁN KARLSSON

TWAYNE PUBLISHERS, INC., NEW YORK
&
THE AMERICAN-SCANDINAVIAN FOUNDATION

PT7511.T45 I513 1967
Thorbergur Thordarson,
1889-1974.
In search of my beloved.

The Library of Scandinavian Literature
Erik J. Friis, *General Editor*

Volume 1

In Search of My Beloved, by Thorbergur Thordarson

Copyright © 1967 by The Library of Scandinavian Literature

MANUFACTURED IN THE UNITED STATES OF AMERICA

Contents

Introduction	7
The Great Exaltation	21
In Outer Darkness	24
To the Land of My Dreams	34
In the Land of Reality	40
Departure	43
The Hour of Parting	46
Off to Siglufjord	52
A New Fragrance	58
Lyrical Days	60
Akureyri	64
Tryggvi from Eyjafjord	68
Romantic Days	79
Dead Days	84
Fruitful Nights	89
On the Move	95
Passing By	106
Oblivion	117
Finis	119

Introduction

THORBERGUR THORDARSON, Icelandic poet, essayist, parodist, storyteller, polemist, folklorist, grammarian, and autobiographer, was born in 1899, on a farm in the outlying district of Sudursveit in the southeastern corner of Iceland. It is a district famed both for its strong traditions and for its natural beauty, lying as it does on a narrow, green strip of land between Europe's largest glacier, Vatnajökul, and the North Atlantic to the south. Without unduly emphasizing the influence of scenery on a country's inhabitants, one must agree that this is a landscape to excite the romantic imagination. Thordarson has presented an extremely vivid and detailed account of his youth in a series of autobiographical works which began with *Steinarnir tala* (The Stones Are Talking, 1956). There are many references, as well, in his earlier writings, to the special influences of his early youth. One of the most powerful of these influences was supernaturalism, the belief in the ubiquitous presence of ghosts, elves, monsters of lake and sea, trolls and magic. To this day Thordarson is a passionately superstitious man in the tradition of his forefathers. Education and the more sophisticated attitudes of spiritualism have failed to change or even modify to a noticeable extent the traditional beliefs of his youth.

I do not think that one can easily exaggerate the importance of these and other romantic elements in Thordarson's artistic character. I should like to suggest that, without them, his humor, his painstaking logicality, comic or serious, and his intense rationalism would have no real point of departure nor any vitality. I do not, however, mean to imply that Thordarson is insincere, for his passionate attachment to truth as he sees it, however absurd it may seem to some of his contemporaries, is beyond question. But, like the true artist that he is, he is undoubtedly aware of his need for these elements. To a great extent they form the basis of his self-mockery, his special manner of poking fun at himself.

In his native language, Thordarson is a great stylist, a magnificent polemist, and a fine storyteller. He is both a traditionalist and innovator in language, a lyric poet, and a rollicking, irreverent parodist in verse. He is a theosophist and a socialist, an activist in politics and a practitioner of yoga, a supernaturalist and a rationalist, a highly credulous man with a scientific turn of mind. As a writer, he will escape simple classifications because ultimately his distinction rests upon a unique personality. It was in the humorous exploitation of this personality that he found his true genre as an artist.

A recurrent image in Thordarson's reminiscences of his early youth is the romantic vision of distant white sails on a blue sea. In those days the French used to send fishing boats up to the coast of Iceland. Quite simply, this vision excites the boy's longing, his desire to get away, his love of things distant or exotic. At the same time, one feels, the image reflects, in its simplicity, Thordarson's lifelong desire for simple perfection. For he has never outgrown or discarded the romanticism of his youth. Later it would find expression in his love of oriental philosophy and yoga, his sincere belief in a socialistic utopia, his passionate involvement with Esperanto on which he spent, according to his own account, six years of his life. All these beliefs and attachments Thordarson has defended with a fierce polemistic rationalism and a superb command of argument whenever the occasion has presented itself.

But the practical effects on the boy's mind of the vision of white sails was to arouse in him the ambition to become a sea captain. With this purpose in mind, he hired out as a cook on a fishing boat from Reykjavik. It was a disappointing experience and a short one. In a different sense, however, it became a long-lasting episode in his life for he was to exploit it in his reminiscences with high comic effect. (e.g. *Íslenzkur aðall*, 1938). In his usual manner, he pictures with swift unsentimental strokes the contrast between the low, thankless existence of the cook (commonly addressed as that "god-damned mud cook") and his humble idealism. His stay on the boat, while dampening his material ambitions, increased his spiritual hunger.

Much of Thordarson's early life was spent in a rather haphazard search for a means of livelihood; he was at various times a day laborer, a house painter, and an indigent bohemian in Reykjavik. Having received little or no formal education, he was nevertheless consumed by varied and often contradictory interests. At one time he attended the Teachers College in Reykjavik, but he did not like it well enough to continue. Later he planned to enter the Latin School, in preparation for the University, but failed in his examination.

Apparently, his failure was to a large extent due to a general feeling of inferiority caused by insufficient schooling, poverty, and real or imagined bad health. Incidentally, Thordarson's hypochondria has served him as a rich source of humor. But his disappointment was soon alleviated by his admittance, on an irregular basis, to the University of Iceland in the fall of 1913. This was due to the good offices of Björn M. Olsen, professor of Icelandic.

Professor Olsen, the man who befriended Thordarson at this critical point in his life, was a great scholar and probably the foremost authority in his day on early Icelandic and Norwegian literature. There is no doubt that he did much to stimulate the scientific interests and scholarly instincts of his extraordinary student. Besides Icelandic literature and philology, Thordarson took some courses in Gothic and Anglo-Saxon, in Latin and in Greek. He also learned German and English. At the university he seems to have felt at home. He did some independent scholarly work there, particularly on the Prose Edda, altogether these studies were never published. He attended the University for five semesters, until the year 1918 when his mentor, Professor Olsen retired. However, because of his irregular status and lack of required basic schooling, he was not awarded a degree for his labors. Later, his studies led to his being granted a yearly government stipend for notating rare terms and phrases from Icelandic folk speech. This occupied him partially for a long time to come and, over the years, he made many trips, usually on foot, to various parts of the country for the purpose of adding to his collection. To ensure the widest possible collaboration, he published, in 1922, a rather remarkable pamphlet, *Leiðarvísir um orðasöfnun* (A Guide to Word Collecting), which, aside from its practical merits, testifies to Thordarson's scholarly attachment to method and his peculiar meticulousness of mind.

For a full appreciation of Thordarson's style and manner, it is well to keep these qualities in mind because they are present in most of his writing and they add a special piquancy to his humorous fancy.

Thordarson contributed to the standard Icelandic dictionary, *Íslenzk-dönsk orðabók* by Sigfús Blöndal and, no doubt, his collection will be of importance for future dictionaries. Of special interest for his personal development is the fact that during his word-collecting trips, he gained an extensive and intimate knowledge of the Icelandic language and speech, of Icelandic folk myths and thought. It is doubtful that any other Icelandic writer possesses such empathetic understanding of native folkways. True to his natural superstitiousness, he has been particularly interested in myths and folk tales of the supernatural. Between 1928 and 1936 he edited, in collaboration with Professor Sigurdur Nordal, a folk tale periodical called *Gráskinna* (Grayhide). *Gráskinna* has recently been reissued in two handsome volumes, with a number of additions, under the title of *Gráskinna hin meiri* (The Greater Grayhide). It is unquestionably, as far as both content and style go, the finest modern collection of Icelandic folk tales. Thordarson's intense interest in tales of the supernatural is reflected in many of his works.

During those early years when Thordarson attended lectures at the University and for some time after, it appeared likely that he might devote himself to the study of language and folk culture. But the spiritual hunger and mysticism which is among his pervasive characteristics as a man and a writer turned his mind early to more esoteric lore, to the study of oriental philosophy, theosophy, and spiritualism. And, at the same time, his rational bent, coupled with strong didactic and reformist tendencies, was increasingly directing him towards the consideration of social problems. About the year 1921, he became, in his own words, "a fiery red socialist." But until 1924, when he published his first important work, *Bréf til Láru* (A Letter to Laura), he had written very little for publication. Two very small volumes of his poetry had appeared, the first in 1914, the second in 1915. These had been reissued in a single volume in 1922, and entitled *Hvítir hrafnar* (White Ravens). Already these poems express a characteristic dual attitude. Personal, romantic lyrics mingle with raucous parodies of the sentimental, melancholy poetic fashion of the time. These parodies express the author's contempt for vagueness and sentimentality as well as his penchant for self-mockery. For he had himself written some excruciatingly conventional poetry in the self-indulgent manner of contemporary Icelandic verse.

A Letter to Laura is a potpourri of opinions, styles, and forms. It purports to be a letter to a real woman, about anything whatever. Actually, it is a collection of articles, stories, parodies, stylistic experiments, folk tales, sermons, autobiography. It was written with great verve and high spirits, exultantly defying affectation of style. In the autobiographical passages, it was startlingly frank and self-revealing in a fashion novel to Icelandic literature. Above all, these passages shone with a kind of humor and self-mockery that was to become Thordarson's unique trademark as an artist.

To many people, *A Letter to Laura* remains Thordarson's greatest work. Its freshness and novelty were, indeed, striking and its style came to influence much of Icelandic writing to this day. It had a profoundly liberating effect on a national literature which was going stale with a rather thin and pallid contemporary convention in prose. Particularly important was the book's influence on a young writer by the name of Halldor Kiljan Laxness who was soon to become Iceland's foremost novelist and a Nobel Prize winner. To be sure Laxness, who was a Catholic at the time, took offense at Thordarson's references to the Catholic Church and wrote a pamphlet in refutation. But the effect of Thordarson's fresh and vivid style on Laxness' writing is beyond question.

By and large, *A Letter to Laura* provoked much criticism because of the author's political and religious views. To these attacks Thordarson responded with a polemical zeal and combativeness that was to characterize much of his later journalistic writing. Also, the book had other and more direct consequences for his career. For some years he had held teaching positions at two trade schools in Reykjavik. On the appearance of *A Letter to Laura*, he was dismissed from both these jobs on grounds of radicalism and anti-church attitudes. Later, Thordarson taught for a period at a high school in Reykjavik but, since the early thirties, he has devoted his entire time to writing.

A Letter to Laura contained the elements of most of Thordarson's later writing, learned, journalistic and autobiographical. His personal style had already evolved: a lucid, spare, classical style, composed of short, rhythmic incisive sentences. It was a superb polemical style but also one that would serve excellently for comic autobiography by imparting a rational, veracious manner to romantic imaginings and neurotic fancy. The risk in pursuing this style, so free from affectation, towards some ultimate perfection was that of making simplicity itself an affectation. There occur in Thordarson's work rare passages that suggest a sort of Basic Icelandic. But the very rarity of such passages tends to remind one of the habitual clarity and expressiveness of his style.

For many years to come, Thordarson's work was limited mainly to journalism and polemics. For a while in the thirties, he contributed regularly to the Social-Democratic paper, *Althydubladid*. During that period, he published two major polemic works, *Althjoðamál og málleysur* (Universal Languages and Non-languages, 1933), in defense of Esperanto, and *Rauða hættan* (The Red Danger, 1935), a political essay. In these critical and journalistic writings, he achieves, almost infallibly, great polemical virtuosity. Through most of them there runs a strain of intense didacticism combined with humor which has reminded some readers of the polemical writings of George Bernard Shaw. To be sure, Thordarson will be found to lack Shaw's intellectual scope. All the same, a comparison might not be altogether to his disadvantage. He would not be found wanting in mental vigor or lucidity of argument. He has, furthermore, the charm of a certain homeliness and warmth which many people might consider preferable to Shaw's cold intellectuality. At any rate, the great Anglo-Irishman who wrote for a world audience and the obscure Icelander who has written so persistently for less than two hundred thousand people have in common a passionate desire to set the world right by means of intellectual argument. As a "Shavian" polemist, Thordarson has added a new dimension to Icelandic literature.

In 1938, Thordarson published *Íslenzkur aðall* (An Icelandic Aristocracy), his first book-length autobiographical work. *In Search of My Beloved* is a translation of the central episode of this book. It is a novella by itself.

For the rest, the book describes the adventures of a group of literary bohemians, in the year 1912, who are trying to make their fortunes during the brief herring season in the north-coast town of Akureyri. *In Search of My Beloved* presents Thordarson's major image, The Unattainable Woman, who is, aside from the personality of the author, the central figure of his reminiscences. The woman's romantic figure and her distant lover's critical self-appraisal form the essential elements of Thordarson's autobiography. For the great romanticist was also a born rationalist with a scientific turn of mind and an innate need for relentless self-observation. What he observed struck him as highly comic and, when he began to exploit his personality in writing, his readers found it even more amusing than he did himself. At his best, he gives the distinct impression of not knowing how funny he is. For, if he belongs in any class at all as a humorist, it is with that rare breed of artists known as *grands naifs*.

Not that his humor is unconscious; on the contrary, he exploits it with great virtuosity. But it is essentially a kind of exaggerated or excessive sanity that strikes the reader as absurd. It means dealing with experience at what appears to be an abnormally close range, overlooking any accepted or general solution to even the minutest of problems. It pursues the analytical process ad absurdum, thus achieving a double fun by mocking both the object under observation and the analytical attitude itself. It is an example of approaching a problem with a fresh eye and also a more or less unconscious parody of the "fresh eye." For, if Thordarson, the polemical and political writer, is a relentless critic of conventional values as well as an unflinching advocate of a pristinely naive rationalism, Thordarson the artist gives both sides their due. His autobiographical protagonist, the *grand naif*, the truth-seeking rationalist, is, to be sure, as a being a living criticism of his fellow men and a constant threat to their existence. But most of his comic misfortunes stem not from his rationalism but from his romantic and irrational follies. In that fashion the author identifies himself most profoundly with his fellow men and therein lies the greatness of his art. But a good deal of the fun is to be found precisely in those scenes where the protagonist discovers the value of conventional attitudes as a means to rational action. Still, he is by nature doomed to be an outsider. Perhaps the best definition of his predicament is the title of his second book of autobiography, *Ofvitinn* (2 vols., 1940-41). It means something like "the fool genius" or, perhaps better: "the simpleton by reason of his gifts."

After *An Icelandic Aristocracy* Thordarson has done mainly narrative writing. There is, for instance the curious and peculiarly Icelandic *Ævisaga Árna Thórarinssonar* I-IV (1945-50). These are the memoirs of an old country parson who happened to be a splendid wit and an inexhaustible storyteller. For Thordarson he had the additional virtue of believing in manifestations of the supernatural: ghosts, elves, monsters. Thordarson acts as a scribe to the parson and the two achieve a particularly happy cooperation. The book turns into a fascinating catch-all of Icelandic folk myths and humor. *Sálmurinn um blómið* (The Hymn to the Flower, 2 vols., 1954-55) purports to be the record of the author's conversations with a child. During the course of the book he manages to cover a great many subjects, including world politics, which seem a bit far-fetched for his young conversant, to say the least. This is, perhaps, the only one of Thordarson's works which tends to become boring, lapsing as it does into prolonged imitations of baby talk. It contains, however, passages of superb narrative humor. One keeps hoping that Thordarson will continue the reminiscences of his youth which, as I mentioned earlier, he has been publishing intermittently since 1956. If he does not, one should not complain, for he has done much and most of that he has done supremely well.

Kristján Karlsson

IN SEARCH OF MY BELOVED

The Great Exaltation

THIS STORY, which the hand of death so harshly brought to an end, as it does so many stories, began in reality a good quarter of a century ago. It was just before midnight one evening in February in the year 1912 and I was walking up High Street on my way home from town. That evening was one of the rare occasions in those days when the glories of the heavens were able to raise man's soul above the realization that it was buried in a pitiful city of ugly buildings with corrugated iron walls, open sewers and muddy walks which bound together the pure of heart. Not a hair on my head stirred. The air was charged with tropical mildness, the sky was sparkling in its clearness, the moon full.

When I reached No. 3 High Street I paused briefly in my walk, leaned up against a rotten telephone pole and began to study the firmament, which that evening glistened with thousands of suns in all colors of the spectrum.

I had not rested my mind long on the silent heavens' play of glittering rays before I was seized by a rapture that was a mixture of great exaltation and poetic weakness. I could feel that something strange and wonderful was on the move somewhere deep in the depths of my consciousness. It was as if everything were falling apart or crashing together in some unendingly mighty, indescribably gentle harmony which was as nothing but yet contained all. And before I realized what was happening a fully formed stanza which I felt would ultimately become a long poem came to my lips:

> Autumn night. The heavens grow dim.
> Pale shadows stroke the brow of earth.
> Still grow the poet's songs of mirth.
> Soft breezes sing a gentle hymn.
> And the earth — she nods in pure white shrouds
> and dreams of spring.
> The sun sinks low behind somber clouds.

After some exertion I pulled myself out of this poetic nightmare, dashed madly home to my room so that the spirit would not leave me, tore my clothes off, jumped into bed, grabbed paper and pencil and finished the poem that night.

It was with such solemnity that the spirit of poetic inspiration came to young men in the last years of peace. He who does not remember those days has never tasted of eternity.

The next morning I began the rewriting, one draft after another. Only the first verse remained unchanged. The voice of the eternal can never be improved upon. The next days passed in showing this gift from heaven to my nearest friends. They learned the poem and said that I was a great poet.

The news spread through the city with the speed of a vicious rumor. Young men who in those days stood in every doorway on the lookout for poets and philosophers now streamed from all directions to No. 10 High Street and asked to speak with or just see this young genius who was not only a poet but in addition a great philosopher and an extreme eccentric and who lived in such romantic poverty that one moonlit evening he had gone down to the seashore to commit suicide because he didn't have a decent pair of shoes. But his feet had gotten so cold as he walked on the slimy beach in his shoes with holes in their soles that he had not been able to commit suicide.

There was no mistaking it. This was genius. Thus had its dignity imprinted itself in the consciousness of young people in the first and second decades of this century: tremendously gifted, completely different, continually broke, hopelessly pessimistic, leaning against telephone poles while others slept, blowing his nose in his sock because he couldn't afford a handkerchief, not able to drown himself because his feet were cold. One admirer, later to become a well-known journalist, loitered days on end beside a telephone pole on High Street with his eyes raised imploringly to the poet's window, which overlooked the outhouse next door.—Ah, yes, it was wonderful to be a poet and a wise man in those days.

That poem was entitled "Night" and was printed at the top of the first page of the newspaper that same spring. And you can understand that that was no small thing for the author if you keep in mind that era's reverence for the printed word. To see one's own poem in the local paper was as much a world event as when an Icelander nowadays is interviewed in a paper in Denmark or England, where all the readers are capable of evaluating great thinking.

In Outer Darkness

THE MEMORY of it is as fresh in my mind as if it had happened yesterday.

It was Wednesday the twelfth of May, and the year was 1912. Cloudy in the morning, then partly cloudy, and clouding over again toward evening. Stiff northwest breeze, then light breeze, and once again stiff breeze. Cool. Sunny. Wakening spring over the slumbering world.

A little past eight o'clock I started up out of an indistinct dream in which I seemed to be standing in front of the broken bit of mirror which hung on the wall to the left of the window, looking at myself.

What do I see?

A bald strip the length of my head from forehead to neck.

I shuddered. Then it seemed as if a voice spoke to me out of the mirror:

"This is only the beginning."

I grabbed at several locks of hair hanging down over my brow. They came loose in my fingers.

Oh, my God! Am I going to loose my thick reddish-blond hair?

And a stench of decay and rot rose from these bits of dead hair.

I tore open my eyes, seized by an icy, convincing suspicion. I tried unsuccessfully to make myself believe that this dream was not the prophecy of hidden powers, the harbinger of a horrid drama.

I jumped out of bed, dressed in a second, poured water into the basin and began to shave. Just precisely today I needed to be irresistibly handsome. My happiness, my life could depend on it. It could mean my salvation.

But then I found to my consternation that the razor was dull, there was nothing to hone it with in the room, no shaving cream, no hot water, and that my beard had become thick and bristly. I hadn't shaved since Saturday morning when I had gone to Hafnarfjord with her. Such is the foresight, the worldly wisdom of a genius.

But I swore I'd get rid of it anyway. So I began to hack away at each whisker separately. I covered my face with bleeding scratches, raged against the misfortune that had descended upon me, took off patches of skin here and there, ground my teeth, cursed out loud, moaned, called on the Savior of mankind, and hardened myself again. And finally, when this vicious battle with my beard was at an end, my torn and bleeding face glowed back at me from the mirror like a full moon rising in back of an erupting volcano.

And just at that moment several hasty, frivolous knocks came at the door. Before I could collect my senses and call out "Come in" the door flew open and she stepped into the room.

"Well, here I am to say goodbye. So long, and thanks for this winter."

Utter confusion. "Uh—uh—uh—wha—wha—uh——? S-s-so long. Are you leaving right away? All I have to do is wash the soap off."

"Well, I have to hurry. The ship is just about to leave."

And she shot out of the door and slammed it after her.

I stood there nailed to the floor and gaped stupidly at the closed door. It grew dark in the room. It was as if a huge paw had wiped all worldly light out of this poverty-ridden dwelling-place, out of my life, out of eternity, at the moment she rushed out the door.

I had never imagined that the parting of two lovers could be like this. I had pictured it in my mind as fervid, burning, full of solemn caresses, pregnant with tender promises of longed-for reunions.

What did it all mean, anyway? Was she really in such a rush? Or was it just a trick to get rid of me? Was it a clever pretence to hinder that I accompany her on board?

Why?

Doesn't she love me?

Perhaps she despises me. Maybe she is ashamed to be seen with me in public.

Or isn't it rather just the opposite? Doesn't she love me so much that she wanted to get this heartrending hour of parting over with as quickly as possible? Or perhaps she was afraid that she wouldn't have been able to hide how intensely she loves me. Maybe she was afraid she would have cried if she had had to bid me farewell over and over again out in public on a ship that never seemed to be able to make up its mind to depart. And it's always embarrassing to cry in public.

I couldn't decide what I ought to believe. All I knew was that we were parted and that my suffering was unbearable. Before I realized it I was restlessly pacing back and forth, from the window to the door, from the door to the window, monotonously, like the shuttle in a loom. Oh, Lord! The weight of my loneliness was crushing. The world was empty and desolate now that she had left. The darkness was overwhelming, the silence bottomless, the desolation unending, my surroundings transformed beyond recognition. I had been cast into outer darkness.

Finally it was as if I caught sight of a faint glimmer of light somewhere farthest in the darkness of my soul. I staggered over to the basin and washed the soap off my face. Then I lurched down the stairs and out of the house.

I paid no attention to where I was going. I wandered around for what seemed an eternity, through countless streets and alleys and squares. I saw nothing, understood nothing. It was as if I were walking in circles in an airtight dungeon somewhere beyond the limits of existence. In outer darkness all paths become as one.

Suddenly I found myself standing on the hillside overlooking the harbor. I had no idea how I had gotten there. I stood there with my smarting, swollen face turned toward the fleet of ships lying at anchor in the shimmering harbor spread out at my feet. But I saw it all only in isolated fragments, heard only snatches of sound, comprehended only detached bits. Here and there the sun glistened on a graceful bow. The sound of a motor. The squeaking of a windlass. The sputtering of a pump. Somewhere in the distance a clock struck: one, two, three . . . high noon. A winch screeched. An anchor chain rattled. I started up. Is the *Western Seas* weighing anchor? Yes, there it is! Hasn't it left before now? Is the truth thus when men love? No, rather in spite of that they love. There must have been a delay in loading. Or the captain was drunk. I felt that the *Western Seas* was the most beautiful ship in the harbor, the proudest ship in Iceland, the most blessed ship in the world.

The sun gleamed on the anchor when the winch had drawn it up out of the fresh water of the sea. Then the propeller began to whip the water into foam. Four blasts of the whistle. And that being done, the ship headed straight for the open sea, powerful, determined, merciless, farther and farther away for each moment. The happy figures of the passengers on the decks melted slowly together into indistinct, formless clumps until they faded into the distance as shadows before the rising sun. And her figure was one of them. Finally there was nothing left except the eternal, which never comes and never goes: the vast expanse of the sea, the islands in the sea and the mountains ringing the sea.

But all ships that depart must someday return . . .

In a few days the *Western Seas* would sail into Hrutafjord under a clear sky, in sparkling sunshine and gentle breezes. The sun is always shining there where one's beloved is. And the young men on the farms along the fjord come running out into the yards and peer at the *Western Seas* through telescopes.

Is she aboard?

Of course she is! There she is, standing beside the steward up on the bridge.

Can't you see the white lace on the sleeves of her blouse?

I just bet she's spent the winter studying in Reykjavik.

And then begins a summer of riding trips on spirited horses over the hills and through the vales. And there are pauses to rest the horses in the deepest vales . . .

Oh, my God! I stumbled down off the hill above the harbor and drifted, sobbing, along the docks. I wandered about town that afternoon like a ghost that can't find its grave.

Late in the day I found myself once more in the center of town. Flags were everywhere, all flying at half mast.
Is someone dead?
Who's dead?
Has the *Western Seas* gone down? Did it run onto a hidden reef? No survivors.
No. It was just King Frederik the Eighth. He had died in Hamburg the evening before. He had died because he could not have the woman he loved. Kings and beggars never get the women they love.

The next few weeks I was constantly in flight before the assaults of an army of memories. I had no peace, and could nowhere find a moment's rest for my soul. I got up at the break of dawn and retreated to some desolate spot outside of the city. There I ran back and forth over windswept hills and grassless plains, day after day in the outer darkness of desperation, monotonously humming or singing out loud with great sensitivity mournful songs of longing.

Towards evening I would return to the city and the streets became the scene for my anguish. I followed a street to its end, swung into the lane that connected it with the next street over, followed that until it led to an alley that brought me onto another street which led to another lane, again and again, over and over, restlessly I plodded along the same muddy gutters until the morning sun cast its shimmering rays into the fleeing corpse of my soul. Perhaps some unexpected salvation is awaiting me on the next street. Perhaps the light of my life is just at this very moment calling to me from the next lane. Who knows but that I still may be able to find some tracks after her blessed feet at the corner of the lane and the next alley. Or maybe the *Western Seas* has just sailed into the harbor and she is aboard because she hasn't been able to live without me. I rush down the street toward the harbor.

Sometimes I was seized by an irresistible desire to track down my friends on the streets and start up lofty conversations on some learned subject or other, for example, the inaccuracy of the compass, the periodic system or the supernatural birth of Our Lord Jesus Christ. I discovered that wisdom and knowledge were the enemies and destroyers of love, while poetry and art were oil on the flaming waters of passion. I could turn myself in an instant into a gale of intellectual brilliancy and hold myself hovering in the jetstream of inspiration. I radiated wisdom. It was as if the gates of a heavenly sluice had been opened. All problems became transparent, I understood everything and the words flowed from my lips as lightly as the carefree dance steps of a sexless maiden. And when the conversation was ended I stepped cleansed and refreshed from the waters of wisdom, raised high above all worldly desires, sensual verses, pangs of love and thoughts of marriage.

But only for a moment.

Then out of the host of memories rose some shrill sentence from the winter before, some unsolved riddle from our hours together, some tempting opportunity that I had not been bold enough to use to best advantage.

Why did she tell me she was trembling one time as I was just about to leave her in the darkness in front of her door in the middle of the night? She scared me to death and I wasn't able to get a bit of sleep all night. I was afraid she might be getting pneumonia. In those days pneumonia always began with trembling.

But then she didn't get pneumonia after all, and the

next evening she came home suspiciously late from her piano lesson. That evening she didn't complain about any trembling and began to tease me by calling me Toby. When that didn't bother me she called me Tubby-Toby.

Thus the days dragged slowly by, indistinguishable from the darkness of suffering, and the darkness of suffering indistinguishable from the snail-like passage of the days.

My most deadly enemy during that bitter war of memories, however, was the house under whose roof the light and shadows of seven months had alternately filled our two hearts. I never entered its door except to catch a few moments sleep or gulp down a few bites of food.

She was sitting over there in that empty corner the first time I saw her, newly-arrived in town, quiet and attentive, with the innocent blush of country life on her cheeks, behind which, however, hid an inner person not quite so closely related to the innocence of country life.

On this now silent staircase I first heard her footsteps like the breath of a new morning of life. It was in the evening, and she had come upstairs.

Here on this bare wooden table she had spread forth two dazzling white silken hands right before my eyes and then drifted off in her thoughts. And I did nothing, just stared down at my burning breast. It was then that temptation's poison first spread itself through my blood.

There she had looked at me with questioning eyes.

And there she had bored her brilliant eyes deep into my soul.

And from here a flashing, seductive glance.

From against this wall shone her gentle smile.

She sat on this sofa when she stretched her right foot forth from under the edge of her skirt and the compass needle of my heart dipped straight toward her big toe.

She was standing in the shadow in that corner when she called me "Honey" once. Maybe she was trying to decide if it would be all right to say just a little more.

But after that she never called me "Honey" any more.

There in front of the stove she stood the evening she twisted her full, soft lips and let out a shrill, cold laugh. I stared at her. What was she laughing at?

She sat beside this window and quietly and sadly sang a melancholy song out at the street. I could hear that the words were about an unhappy girl whom men didn't understand. Who didn't understand whom? And I said to myself in all the purity of my heart: How can a young and healthy girl who has enough money to pay punctually for herself the first of each month be so ungrateful toward life as to sing such a sad song?

That time she said she was trembling she paused just a second before this door, quietly grasped the handle and cast a glance over her shoulders to me. Then she disappeared alone into the darkness behind the door. And I tiptoed up the stairs thinking about pneumonia.

In through this door she came with a shawl over her shoulders and dressed in a colorful dress the first time she called me Toby. And one lovely moonlit evening a little later she stood all dressed up in front of the full-length mirror over there on the wall, with swelling breasts and a white silk veil over her shoulders and white lace around her beautifully formed girlish wrists. She was on her way to the first school dance. I hated school dances. Text for the evening: The sufferings of a great man from the Book of Youth. The clock struck three. Just after that I heard someone walking around downstairs. I thought the dance was supposed to be over at one o'clock . . .

Gradually, however, the memories took on another hue as the events of the winter grew more distant. They slowly settled to the bottom of my soul and arranged themselves there in orderly tonal rows which resonated like a deep and quieting, slightly melancholy and mystic accompaniment to my disorderly and distraught consciousness of daily life. They bestowed upon me a new sense of the fullness of existence, painted the vistas of my perception with new colors and gave the work of my hands deeper meaning.

Little by little I found I could once more turn my thoughts to the hopelessness of the struggle of life, which was now all tied up with the old problem:

Where can I find some work?

Finally I succeeded in panning my frailty off on the State Highway Department. There was road work up north in Hrutafjord.

And the days marched through the city mildly and graciously and disappeared in the evenings into the golden hall of the west like holy Buddhas extinguishing the work of a lifetime in the realm of darkness.

To the Land of My Dreams

WE WERE SEVERAL young men from Reykjavik who started out for Hrutafjord aboard the good ship *Ingolfur* a little past nine o'clock the morning of the eighth of June. The boat trip up to Borgarnes was marvelous. The bay was covered with gentle, nonchalantly rippling waves. The mountains rose amiably on the horizon. The sun was swathed in an almost tropical bank of clouds. The mildness and dignity of spring lay over land and sea.

I was sitting off by myself up on deck, lost in thought. The mood of enchantment evoked by my surroundings led my thoughts to an old song that I had heard for the first time in similar weather on these same waters five years before. I was at that time cook on the fishing smack *Hafsteinn* and we were sailing into the bay. It was around midsummer. The spring fishing season was at an end.

It was late in the morning, during the short watch. I had just finished scraping and scrubbing a two-week-old crust of filth off the cabin floor, doused it with bucket after bucket of water and swept the whole mess into the anchor room under the floor. The floor shone up at me dazzling white, framed by the smoky, blue walls colored by the acidic stench of many bountiful seasons.

I returned to my stove and tended to the huge kettle

of fish boiling over a crackling fire. The crew would kill me if the fish wasn't just right . . .

It was a peaceful, quiet Sunday and up on the deck several young sailors were holding a leisurely conversation about the graceful little sailboats they swore they would climb aboard as soon as they got off this damned stinking tub. But suddenly a lull came in the conversation and two bright young voices broke into a resounding song that shattered the peaceful passage of the ship:

> I'm off across the Seven Seas
> to the land where my sweetheart dwells;
> I'm off across the Seven Seas
> to the land where my sweetheart dwells:
> Behind the mountains and valleys deep
> On the green and grassy plain.

I listened enthralled. I had never heard such a bewitching song before. Such a full and powerful melody had never before reached my ears. I felt as if every note, every single word (with the exception of that stupid "plain") went straight to the deepest roots of my heart. And when the final tones had died on the lips of the singers it was as if the contents of my soul had been turned upside-down. That which before had faced up, now faced down and that which before had pointed downwards, now pointed upwards. My gift for mathematics, my desire to measure and discover, my love of geology—all heritages from home—sank in a single instant to the murky depths of my soul never to rise again. But at the same instant there shot to the surface of my soul a feeling of romantic intoxication, a love of abstract thinking, a lyrical tension in my nerves and an infallible sense for rhyme. And behold! My eyes were opened and I perceived a new dimension. The blue dimension.

It was only the word "plain" that cast a tiny discordant shadow over this rich and colorful revelation. Why not rather:

> On the green and grassy slope.

And I suddenly saw my beloved before me, spending the summers working on a farm at the base of a long, grassy slope. In the calm, pale-blue evenings she sits far up the slope and thinks about a fair-haired lad who lives by himself in a room in the attic of a tiny house. I was red-haired and shared a room with two others.

I sat with bowed head there on the bench beside the stove for a long time and gazed in pure ecstasy straight through the cabin floor and the anchor room into this new, magnificent world. The crackling of the fire, the boiling of the water and the whining of the teakettle grew more and more distant, became unreal and faded out somewhere far, far off. They did not belong in this new dimension.

"Hasn't that damned cook begun to dish it out yet?" thundered a voice down through the hatch at the same time as a pair of revolting sea boots thumped down the iron ladder up by the stove. "Where the hell is he, anyway? Goofin' off, I bet."

"Give him a good swift one. It's almost four bells and he's not called us in yet," another voice shouted down from the deck.

I started up, dragged suddenly and violently down to the banal plane of pots and teakettles. And when I looked into the pot the fish was boiled to pieces.

And the tea was undrinkable swill.

"We oughta give it to him good, the damn little fool."

"Let's pour a few buckets over him and see if we can snap him out of it."

"And he's not even ashamed! Look at the silly grin on his face. A hell of a cook!"

That was my first rebirth.

Thus began my misfortunes. That simple little song was the prelude to a life of suffering.

Perhaps I wouldn't be sitting here on the deck now if those sailors had just kept up their incomprehensible talk about graceful sailboats instead of beginning to sing about sweethearts far off beyond mountains and valleys across the Seven Seas. People should be careful what songs they sing when youngsters can hear.

We stopped ashore in Borgarnes at 1:30 P.M. and spent the rest of the afternoon making preparations for the journey further. Close to six o'clock we started up the road on foot with two horse-drawn wagons and three spare horses.

The trip north passed without event. All the events took place afterwards. Each day the sun shone brightly and exhausted from the heat we arrived at the farm which would provide us with lodgings for the night. Early the next morning we would start off again with stiff and aching muscles. Each evening before I went to bed I staggered out of the farmyard and thought beautiful thoughts about my beloved.

Then finally on Tuesday the eleventh of June, around two o'clock, we had a view north from the heights that separate northern and southern Iceland. Hrutafjord lay spread out before us like a calm sea of mist on a clear summer morning. I was amazed at how near it looked, it was as if we were standing on the edge of a cliff from which we would tumble into the waves. But the cliff receded slowly from the water as we threaded our way carefully along innumerable narrow paths down the slope at the foot of which the land of my dreams stretched itself farther and farther out with its silvery fjord and low, colorless clumps scattered here and there on the hills. Those were the farmhouses. I was touched that they were so small. On small farms live people who read books and think about the welfare of their souls. And true love flowers nowhere but there. Only there are to be found pure maidens who give away their hearts only once and never take it back through all eternity. But on large farms live greedy people who never look in books, have never loved anything except money and themselves, who sell their hearts to the highest bidder and who walk again after they have died and wander around in the darkness of the underworld until the darkness has taught them to love as do the good people who live on small farms.

What would my stay on the shores of this shimmering fjord bring me? Perhaps just new icy blasts off Hell's cold glaciers. Maybe a tiny taste of Heaven followed by life-long Hell. Or possibly a short Hell with a long and serene Heaven in its wake. I asked the powers-that-be to take all these chalices from my lips. I thirsted only for something lovely that would last a reasonable length of time, but yet which would never take end—her heart alone—her snow-white hands through all eternity.

About one o'clock the next day we unhitched the horses, dug four deep holes down into the land of my dreams and set up two shining white Highway Department tents beside the road a short distance from one of the little farms.

A good three hours later I met my beloved at the farm

which was her home, just casually and uneventfully, as when you meet someone in the door in the twilight and say: Well, well, here you are.

I was terribly abashed. All my suffering had been for nothing. All my anguish had been foolish self-deception, a stupid flight from my empty fancy. All my castles-in-the-air about a sun-filled land beyond mist-topped mountains had been nothing but a barbaric lack of honesty with myself. All my speculations about rest pauses in deep vales nothing but naive overestimation of her character. And I had traveled all this way to the Arctic Ocean away from summer and sun for this!

I saw suddenly that this land of my dreams was in reality the ugliest corner of the earth. More than that, I realized that I was no longer the least bit in love with her and couldn't even imagine that I ever had been. Not even the smallness of the farm could cast over her unattractiveness the faintest shimmer of that nobility of heart that pious souls had taught me characterized true love.

"I don't plan to stay here this summer," I said, so that she wouldn't get the idea that it was because of her that I had come north. "I'll be here only until the herring season starts. Then I'm going to Siglufjord. It's a lot more fun in Siglufjord than here. So long!"

But as soon as I had left her I thought I was going to die of a love that was lifted far above the inconstancies of both life and the world of dreams.

In the Land of Reality

UNRELENTING north wind with cloudy skies and low temperatures. We began work at half past six in the morning and lay down our picks and shovels at half past six in the evening. Three times a day we ate rye bread with margarine and four times a day we drank black coffee with old, hardened confectioner's sugar. Then we lay our aching and cold bodies down to sleep on moldy bags of hay and covered ourselves with filthy cotton blankets. The silence of the night was broken only by an occasional weary snore or wheezing sigh.

I never saw my beloved. Six times a day I went off by myself and sang down at my boots: Oh, do you still remember your Alice, Ben Bolt? Who was Alice? Where was Alice? How was Alice? What did Alice die of? Can other girls die of the same thing?

Thus the mighty stream of time rolled by on the western shore of Hrutafjord in June, 1912.

Finally Sunday the sixteenth of June dawned bright and clear, as if the universe had been scrubbed clean during the night. I crawled with stiff and aching muscles out of the sack about nine o'clock, dressed in my best, shaved and inspected myself in the water barrel outside the tent door. Then I set off to visit my beloved.

Oh-ho! Things are going to happen today, I said to myself. Why just today? Hadn't I been telling myself all winter that something would happen today, or tomorrow? And did anything ever happen? I'd say to myself as she sat blushing and warm and eager opposite me at the dinner table: This damned fooling around can't go on any longer. Something's got to happen this evening. Then evening came. We sat alone at the table by the window in my room. I enthusiastically unraveled the mysteries of my astronomical charts spread out on the table before her: This is Vindemiatrix in Virgo and this is Denebola in Leo, both stars of the third magnitude. And look, here's Asellus Borealis and Asellus Australis in Cancer, stars of the fifth magnitude. Wasn't she overwhelmed by my tremendous knowledge? She folded her snow-white hands in the middle of the map and drifted away in her thoughts. Then I said to myself: Oh well, there's plenty of time tomorrow. Thus passed every evening and every tomorrow all winter long. And nothing ever happened. But today I was strong, and I swore by the gods that I would go all out, that something spectacular would happen, before the sun went down. Something *will* happen, I said and clenched my fists.

I ambled along the road by the fjord and was in seventh heaven. I felt myself one with the universe, united with the sunshine, the earth and the heavens. The air was full of the songs of birds and sheep lay chewing their cuds on fragrant, grassy slopes, their eyes half closed, as when one dreams without being aware of it. A brook rippled and glistened gaily farther up the mountainside. And I sang from the abundance of my heart: My hope is kindled in the light of your eyes. That was the theme-song of this glorious morning. And if you travel along that shore a bright summer morning and listen attentively, you may still hear it echoing from hill and dale.

That was perfect bliss.

I was received with open arms. Coffee and cake, food and coffee and once again coffee and cake. Light-hearted conversation that no memory could have reconstructed once the words had left our lips. Diplomatic glances, either into her luscious bedroom or out at sun-filled hollows in the flower-covered fields. Nothing had happened yet. But there was no hurry. There was plenty of time left. When our eyes met in her room we saw someone standing behind them saying: Well, well, something great has to happen when you get outside in the fields out of sight of the house. And when we were seated amidst fragrant buttercups in a hollow out of sight of the house he said: You've got to go to it when you're back inside.

Thus that whole love-clear day of rest went its way. The mighty light of the universe cast the beams of love into our hearts. The hollows in the fields said: You can't be seen from the house here. The key in the lock offered to keep secret life's most longed-for adventure. But still nothing happened. The clock struck six. Oh, well, there'll be plenty of time this fall, I told myself.

Then I stood up from the supper table, extended my thanks and stepped out into the solitude of life.

I was once more alone, helpless, disappointed, repenting. The wellsprings of life had disappeared down into the sandy wastes of my soul. The birds had ceased their singing. Cold blasts of wind came down the mountainside instead of the merry rippling of the brook. And I sang, not giving my heart a second's rest: Take from me my sorrow, ocean deep! Take from me my sorrow, ocean deep!

Thus end all days that begin with love of the ephemeral.

Departure

THE FOLLOWING MORNING my condition dangled before my imagination like a bloody crucifixion scene in a Catholic church. This stinking road work wasn't going to get me anywhere. It brought me only heart-rending longing, thorncrowned agony, irresolute desire that never dares go to action. It produced only the crucifixion of the flesh which yet can never die.

I'll tear myself out of this excruciating Hell, I said to myself. I'll join the herring fleet in Siglufjord, make a lot of money, bury myself in studies next winter and drown all these miserable pangs of love in the well of sexless knowledge. The day I shake the dust of this accursed place from my feet I'll enter a new life, be revitalized, strong, wise and indifferent to the temptations of the flesh.

But unfortunately the circumstances were not just quite right for such a break. It was neither New Year's Day nor my birthday, not even the solstice nor the first of the month, much less the first day of the week, nor even twelve o'clock noon or midnight. This could occasion a new downfall.

It was Saturday the twenty-ninth of June at a quarter to twelve noon that I bid my comrades farewell and set out for Siglufjord. By that time we were working far north along the shore of the fjord. I rented a horse from a farmer and arrived in the town at the inmost arm of the fjord late in the afternoon.

The town was the scene of elections and a fair that day. The place was packed and spirits rose as the evening wore on. The sheriff, the director of the telephone company and the local representative to the Parliament held forcible speeches and when they were finished the dancing began. People hung around in the doorways and looked on, sneaked in and out the doors and through the halls, paired off here and there outside behind houses and sheds, sneaked back in and danced again, hung around in the doorways and looked on.

My beloved was one of the beautiful girls who took part in the festivities. But she was never seen sneaking outside with anyone or talking with a man alone and she danced with no one except her brother. I didn't dance. And she probably thought it would have been improper to dance with anyone except her brother since I wasn't dancing. I looked at her often. How beautiful she was! Dark hair, shining eyes, red lips, flushed cheeks, snow-white hands, a silk shawl, lace ruffles. There'll be plenty of time at midnight, I whispered to myself. Midnight: It's best to wait until two o'clock. I'll be a different man by then. And so I tried to drown my irresoluteness in song and drink. I wonder if she can hear with what deep feeling I'm singing? Finally, when the spirit had become strong and willing, the flesh was weak.

At the dance I met a young red-haired woman with sparkling light gray eyes and an intelligent look about her. She was single, a close relative of my beloved and I found I liked her. Her name was Christine. She seemed to look at me with the air of a sage who knows the laws of life and the secrets of death. She looked at me often and it seemed to me that she was saying to herself: Now he's thinking something deep and wise. This young man has quite a head on him. When we parted she invited me to visit her home the following day. I accepted with pleasure. I knew that my beloved would also be there.

About six in the morning the dance hall was emptied. The dancers caught their horses, saddled them and rode off, some to the south, some to the north. Nothing was left in the town except a few deserted houses that huddled silently together in the damp morning.

The Hour of Parting

IT WAS ONE O'CLOCK in the afternoon before my soul had reentered my body in my room in the town's one hotel. My head was empty for all poetic thoughts. In order to tune my brain cells to the lyrical mood of the day I bought a half bottle of whisky and set off down the road. Here and there along the way I dropped into a grassy hollow, took a swig and thought: She has sat here some sunny spring morning when each blade of grass was covered with shining pearls of dew and whispered to the all-knowing silence: Who will be my love here in life? And she has from this spot gazed at the lonely gull flying over the calm fjord on a quiet August evening. Where is now the gull that was mirrored in those enchanting eyes?

Then I began to sing again. But I did not now sing about hope-kindling eyes that lift you to the heavens, nor about the ocean deep that so mercifully takes to itself the sorrows of men when they are about to perish on the cross of life. I now hummed solemn melodies about the fickleness of fate.

By the time I arrived at my destination the world seemed to be filled with sunshine and summer. My beloved sat all dressed up in her finest in a chair by the window. Her blood was warm and rich. And she had dark gray eyes that shot sparks at me when I opened the door.

Christine radiated vivacity and intelligence. She and I talked together for two hours about the relationship of God and sin while my beloved listened intently.

An Icelandic author had recently advanced the theory that, in contrast with the older dogma of the sharp distinction between the spheres of activity of God and the Devil, God was also in sin. The courage which he had exhibited in not only thinking of, but also putting in print, such a theory had won him the praise of many freethinking men and the animosity of those whose ways of thinking were yet unpolluted by knowledge.

"But to be perfectly honest, my dear Christine," I said as I cast a philosophical gaze deep into my beloved's eyes, "I must add in conclusion that I am not quite in agreement with this good man."

"Oh, what do you find wrong in this theory?"

"In my opinion it is not precisely correct to say that God is *in* sin. God *is* sin, because God is everything."

"Do you then think that God is that manure pile out there by the barn?"

"Why not? What, after all, is that manure pile?"

"The droppings of the cows since last fall."

"Of course. And that is in reality nothing but a new form of the growth which flowered on the fields last summer. And didn't you that time think that all that wonderfully fragrant life was just exactly what you have called God in nature? Tell the truth now."

"Yes, I guess I'll have to admit that I have sometimes entertained such thoughts."

"Good. But is there then anything more sinful in imagining that God *is* the growth of the soil than in imagining that He is *in* said growth. You are nearer to God when you imagine that everything *is* God than when you believe that God is *in* everything and that between you and Him stands some unnoble and impenetrable wall. Now observe: This fall or next spring the manure will be spread on the fields and He will awaken anew all these sleeping treasures of the fields which you call grass and flowers. That is God renewing himself."

"Wouldn't it then be well for us to worship the manure pile as God?"

"That will probably not be directly necessary. But why do you insist on this degrading attitude of worship? A love-struck young man worships the soul of his beloved. He considers her soul to be more gifted, more noble, more loving than all other souls. But why does he worship her soul?"

"Because the soul is the most noble part of man."

"I don't think it is because of this. I think rather that there are two other reasons why he worships her soul. It is, in the first place, the nature of infatuation to magnify the object of a man's love. It is a sort of mist that drifts before the eyes of the soul and distorts everything out of proportion. But the main reason is that the young man doesn't know her soul well enough. Therefore he worships it. Just as men worship God in Heaven. We never worship anything other than that which we do not know and understand. Worship is the ignorance of the frail. When we get to know an individual, whether he is God or a man, we cease to worship him. For then we understand him. And when we understand him we begin to associate with him as a comrade and equal, instead of looking up to him as an obsequious slave. When a lover marries his beloved he gradually ceases to worship her soul because he has begun to know her. It is because of this that most marriages are the most worshipless relationships in the universe."

"Why only most, not all, marriages?"

"Because some married couples are so fortunate that they never get to know each other . . ."

My beloved's shining eyes were fastened on me. How was I to interpret this? Was she *so* impressed by my wisdom? Did she want to walk with me alone out into the fields so as to have a chance to flood me with her enthusiasm for me in the presence of God in nature? But why was she looking at me like *that*? I started. An ice-cold chill ran down my spine. Then the horrible truth dawned on me. This passion of mine to witness for the truth had lured me into a vicious trap. This was not the place. And this was not the time. I blushed all the way to the tips of my toes. How could any honorable girl trust such a creature in matters of love? Does any decent girl choose to be understood rather than worshiped? To have a comrade rather than a slave? An all-seeing philosopher rather than a blind family man? Had I committed an unpardonable sin? Would these inspired hours of conversation be the ruination of my life? Was also this opportunity-laden day to be one of dark and debasing defeat?

I attempted to fumble my way out of this predicament to a more practical and neutral subject for conversation. But I could produce no echo in the room. I heard only my own voice. It was getting late and it was time for me to be leaving if I was to reach the eastern shore of the fjord by evening. My beloved had stood up and was vehemently preparing to leave. I also stood up, thanked Christine for her hospitality and crushed her hand in farewell.

Outside in the yard stood several saddled horses. My beloved intended to accompany me as far as town.

"Accompany you? Don't get any such ideas. I'm going to accompany these friends of mine from out west. You can tag along behind if you wish."

I was really quite pleased with this. It was just as well that we weren't left alone. What is more frustrating than to let the last moments with your beloved slip out of your numb and irresolute hands at the same time that you are listening to your soul whisper to your quivering heart: This is your chance! Why not now? Do you think you'll have a better chance later on? This moment will never return! And perhaps you even hear the dark red flames within your beloved's soul hiss in your ear: I'll despise you the rest of my life if you don't let something happen now.

And still nothing happens.

But when there are other people present you can't be blamed if nothing happens.

Finally the hour of parting came when we arrived in town. It was seven o' clock. In the evening, that is. It was quite cloudy. And the fog was rolling in from the north. We shook hands and said goodbye to each other, she sitting in the saddle, I standing on the ground.

"Goodbye, now."

"Goodbye."

At the same moment she viciously struck her horse with her whip and dashed off with her retinue. She never even looked back. I reeled as if she had dragged the earth from under my feet after her. I stared at her vanishing form. A close-fitting riding jacket. A dark hat with a white veil. A silver-mounted whip in her snow-white hand. Her wide-spread thighs clutching the rhythmically bounding horse. It all disappeared over the brow of the hill.

I have never been able to figure out how I reached the ferry that took me over the fjord. The first I remember was that I arrived at a pretty little farm on a slope on the eastern shore of the fjord. It was there that I spent this unforgettable night.

When I later found myself alone I felt as if everything contained in my soul had dried up—everything except one thing. That was suffering, an all-encompassing, immovable, gloomy suffering, a calm, bottomless well of unchanging agony. There was from one moment to another not the slightest variation, not the least bit of intensification or abatement, not the minutest change. My soul was like a sea of melted lead not bounded by any discernible horizon. I sat motionless and gazed with dull, stiff eyes at the gray wall opposite me.

It was not until sometime long after midnight, when the messengers of sleep had shackled all my feelings, that I could just barely catch sight of a faint glimmering far off in the darkness. There was yet hope. I reached into my pocket and pulled forth my diary and a pencil and scrawled down the following sentences, the unpremeditated record of the darkest hour of my life:

Life is unbearable. I see Death standing before the door of my heart. But *one* hope, faint and half-extinguished, lights up the yet untrod path. But if that hope dies, that path will remain untrod.

What was this faint half-extinguished hope?

That something would happen next fall. That was the hope. And it was this empty consolation that kept me afloat on the sea of life.

Off to Siglufjord

TEN O'CLOCK.

I was standing fully dressed in front of the farmhouse, sniffing the air in all directions as if it were my first day of life on earth. My head was a bit hazy and I felt strange and somewhat groggy. I wasn't quite sure of where I was or what the world about me looked like or, for that matter, whether I was in a world at all. But gradually everything began to grow clear, one perspective after another opened up and the world disclosed itself as it was at the beginning of time: a shining blue sky, dead calm, the pleasant heat of the sun.

The flies buzzed joyfully, sun-filled songs about the house, darted from one gable to another, dozed there in silence a few moments, then flew in sharp twists and turns toward the awaiting manure piles. That was their search for happiness, their hope-filled journeys to sweethearts beyond distant mountains.

The fjord lay shining and clear as ice at the foot of the green slope. On the far side rose up ridges and heaths, backed in the northwest by a mountain. Her mountain. What might she be doing now? What is she thinking about? Whom is she longing for?

This idyll was suddenly disrupted by panic-stricken thoughts of money. I fumbled after my wallet and frantically searched through it. Only a few crowns left! This won't last me half the way to Siglufjord! What's happened to all my money? My memory of the preceding evening contained several blank spaces that I was not, even through the utmost of effort, able to fill in. I stood for a while in utter confusion. Then a light went on. I set out at top speed for the next farm, which lay directly across the fjord from the town. Why not row across the fjord and listen to the voice of memory rise up from the ground which the soles of her feet had imparted with undying speech the night before? Maybe she was even still in town, perhaps she had forgotten something and had to come back. And then maybe the hotel owner's son had invited her upstairs for a cup of coffee. Would that be anything to wonder at? Perhaps I could still find the imprints of her footsteps around the hotel. New soles. High heels. Exuberant steps. She walks as if she has a goal in life.

 I rented a boat at the farm and rowed across the fjord to town, went straight to the store and hit the manager for ten crowns, giving as security some tools I claimed I had left with the road crew. Then I made a bee-line for the hotel and bought a bottle of whisky. Two crowns gone.

 But then for some strange reason I lost all desire to search for the footsteps of my beloved and I even found that it made absolutely no difference to me if she was fighting desperately to defend her innocence in a room right over my head or if she was snuggling repentingly down in a shady hollow out of sight of the farm at the foot of the mountain which so fascinated me when I gazed at it from the other shore of the fjord. I strode with revitalized steps down to the boat, shoved off, grasped the oars and gently and carefully dipped them into the water. To disturb that lovely surface would have been blasphemy, a rudeness toward the sanctity of nature. The plainness of the western shore gradually assumed a romantic air. My beloved began to appear here and there on its banks and slopes, ever restless, ever looking for something. What was she looking for? And how gracefully her feet touched the earth! And how grateful the earth was to feel her weight! I pulled the boat up on the opposite shore.

When the sun stood directly over the little farm where eyes first saw the light of day I set off to the north on a decrepit old nag, the laziest creature I have ever mounted. My destination was Hvammstang in Midfjord, where I would take passage on a boat to Siglufjord. That was the last station in the land of my dreams. When this minute hand had made but one revolution all that was a part of her would be but the shreds of recollection: her mountain, her fjord and also God's heaven over her mountain and her fjord.

I occasionally wetted my lips with whisky to increase my powers of resistance against the cruel blows of this last hour. Every now and then I dismounted, sat down and gazed at the mountains on the other side of the fjord as they glistened in the rays of the afternoon sun. They slowly moved farther and farther off into the distance and cast over me a steadily increasing spell. Finally only one peak was still visible. Her mountain. I dismounted and climbed up a grassy knoll by the side of the road. I sat up there a long time and soaked up every little detail of that peak, every ridge, every tiny cut, every sun-reddened point, every shaded brook course on its face, so that I would be able to satisfy the eye of my soul when the pangs of love called my memory back to this glorious view. Maybe she is also looking up at the mountain at this very moment. Perhaps our eyes are meeting in that little hollow under the ridge.

It now seemed to be such a short distance over to that peak. I felt that it would have been nothing to jump over there. And then come walking down the mountainside. She is sitting in her lovely little room crocheting. The door is not locked. How white her hands are! And how alluring and enticing her fingers!

Suddenly something whispers inside of her: Look out the window. She looks out the window and sees no one. Who whispered: Look out the window? Then the voice inside her says: Look at the man coming down the side of the mountain. She looks up at the mountain and sees a man coming. Who can that be? He comes closer and closer. Now he's approaching the house. No! Can it be true? She tosses her crocheting aside, rushes down the stairs and cries out, without caring the least bit if anyone hears her or not:

"Oh! Thorbergur has come!"

Then she comes running toward me as if I were a deeply loved and longed-for friend who has spent ten long and sorrowful years far away from her. And we meet out in the fields. Out of sight of the house. And now no one is standing behind our eyes saying: Go to it when you get back inside the house . . .

"How wonderful it is that you've returned, my dear beloved friend! Now we'll never more be parted, never, never more."

Never more be parted! I gallantly remounted the nag and turned my back on the mountain. Then began the wearying ride to the promised land.

As I rode along it was as if an invisible wind constantly held my head turned in the direction of the mountain, like a weather-cock on a house-top. The last instant approached with steady steps, foot by foot, unfaltering. One, two, three. And then it rushed down on me like an obliterating landslide. The highest peak of her mountain disappeared behind the ridge.

I dismounted and picked two flowers that were growing on exactly the spot from which I last saw any part of her mountain. I kissed them, first that one that was growing nearer the mountain, then the other, three kisses each. Then I wrapped them in a piece of white paper and put them in my breast pocket over my heart and assumed a noble pose, extended three fingers of my right hand as high towards the all-seeing heavens as I could and solemnly pronounced these words: With this breath, at this instant, I will begin a new life which I herewith dedicate to Wisdom, Love of All Mankind and Will Power. Hear this, see this and know this, ye mighty rulers of the universe: Spirit of Knowledge, Spirit of Love, Spirit of Power. Amen!

But when the last word had died on my lips it was as if a mainspring snapped somewhere near my heart. It reverberated long after far into the most silent corner of my soul. I tore the stopper out of the bottle and drank in long, demented swallows.

To be sure, it was the first of the month. July 1, 1912. But it was Monday and it was long past noon. And I was a fool who could not distinguish between the fickle blue of the distant mountains and the honest light of the eternal present.

Having completed these ceremonies I once more mounted the old nag (though with a bit more difficulty this time) and continued on to the promised land. Everything that was a part of my beloved was now only a memory.

It was almost nine o'clock when I arrived in Hvammstang. I was by that time very drunk and my thoughts most resembled pounding breakers on a rocky shore. But during the next two days my soul once more regained a state of equilibrium. The shrill chorus of memories gradually blended into a soft, pleasant, sad undertone that concealed itself like an old refrain behind every perception of my eyes or ears, every thought of my brain, every feeling of my heart.

But when I began to investigate the causes of this sudden change I discovered that I was deluding and consoling myself again with the hope of eventful and passionate hours of love at number 10 High Street the following fall and winter. I had once more begun to "live in hope." And those who live in hope are sailing rudderless on the stormy sea of life.

Eight o'clock in the morning of Wednesday the third of July the steamer *Vesta* sailed into the harbor. A half hour later I was seated on a sack of smelly fish refuse on the landing boat that would take me out to the steamer.

At ten o'clock *Vesta* sailed out onto the open sea on the way to the promised land.

A New Fragrance

I ARRIVED in Siglufjord for the first time in my life early in the morning of the sixth of July. It was cold and windy and I can still remember how lonely and helpless I felt as I scrambled with my luggage down the ship's ladder, surrounded on all sides by sombre cliffs that extinguished my last ray of hope of ever returning to the sun-filled land of my dreams to the west.

Yet it was still another aspect of my first meeting with Siglufjord that made the deepest impression on my memory. It was the odor that rose up to meet me when I was deposited on the dock at half-past six in the morning exhausted from lack of sleep and an overwhelming disgust for life. I had never before experienced such an odor. It lay in wait in every alley, every street, it oozed through all cracks and chinks and found its way through flesh and bone to lodge itself in the marrow. I felt it as a deep degradation that I, a lyric poet, was now forced to enter such a stinking hole. But my sense of good taste quickly learned to humble itself before its surroundings.

There was no work to be had in Siglufjord. The herring had not yet come and there were no prospects that it would come in the foreseeable future. Those most understanding of the inscrutable ways of fish had even begun to doubt that any herring at all would be caught in Siglufjord that summer. I took these prospects calmly, however, and didn't even feel the slightest regrets that I had given up well paid work in Hrutafjord for this.

While there I met several friends from Reykjavik who had the same attitude toward life as I. They were, as I, looking for work, were penniless and homeless, as I, and, also as I, ate at the Post Office for one crown a day, always on credit.

It was a true joint shipwreck and we tried desperately to save ourselves by forming a sort of philosophical common front against any and all meditations on the blessings of this life. In the daytime we strolled around town or lay flat on our stomachs up on the mountainside and gazed at the gleaming cloud castles that the winds of the heavens raised only to level and then raise still more beautiful ones on the ruins of the first. At night we held to in an old packhouse down by the harbor where the odor of the town was strongest and most unforgettable.

Lyrical Days

SEVERAL DAYS after I had arrived in Siglufjord a herring trawler from Reykjavik tied up at the dock. A short while later two strange birds stumbled up the pier, two elegantly dressed young men about twenty years old, fresh and new-baked as the first man before the great fall in Paradise. The one was large and heavily built, with a short nose and rather small blue eyes, the other thin and long-faced, with a long, curved nose and large gray-blue eyes. The latter limped and used a cane. They stood for a moment on the pier and stared around them, up at the mountains, down at the water, and sniffed the air like two calves let out of the barn into the strange world for the first time in the spring. And when they finally gave up trying to make anything out of this strange world they began to ask everyone they met about Thorbergur Thordarson, the man who had written the poem "Night" which had appeared on the first page of the paper, because they had heard that he had come to Siglufjord. But no one they met knew anyone by this name or had ever read the poem "Night" which had appeared on the first page of the paper. Culture had not yet spread so far north.

"But haven't you seen a hatless man with a huge shock of red hair and a pointed nose who wanders around staring straight up into the air? Look, like this!"

Yes, everybody in Siglufjord had seen this creature and could even tell the newcomers where it could be found.

These two gentlemen who thus suddenly and unexpectedly arrived by trawler in Siglufjord were Gunnar and Thorleif, acquaintances of mine from Reykjavik who had been frequent visitors at my room in No. 10 High Street. They, too, had come to Siglufjord to try their luck on the herring fleet though, to be sure, neither of them had even been close to anything resembling hard work and a live herring was something they had only heard about. They were true children of Reykjavik. They joined our listless band and life went on.

One day, which was quite different from all other days in Siglufjord, the news reached us that a certain Stefan from Whitedale had arrived in town. This man was completely unknown to all of us, but we were fascinated by his name and we were certain that he would turn out to be an unusually interesting person. Some of us guessed that he was a horse trader, others seemed to remember that he was a heartless creditor who was out to close down various businesses in Siglufjord and Eyjafjord. But most of us felt that his name was symbolic and that he must be the proclaimer of the new faith, a reborn man who had transformed to dazzling whiteness something or other in some place or other.

The next day I was lying up in the packhouse reading when someone came with a message to me that Stefan from Whitedale was outside and wished to see me.

So, he's one of them, I thought. He's undoubtedly read "Night". I lay my book aside and went outside. There stood several of my companions and with them a stranger, a tall man, a bit older than I, slightly stoop-shouldered, with a hooked nose and strange staring gray eyes, a protruding lower lip, a high brow and thick blonde hair. He was lame and supported himself with an old cane. We were introduced.

"This is Stefan from Whitedale. And this is Thorbergur Thordarson who wrote the poem 'Night'."

Stefan stared at me as if I had written the greatest poem in the world. Someone mentioned that Stefan was a poet too.

"Where do you come from?" I asked him.

"Just from Hjalteyri now."

"Are you going to be there this summer?"

"I plan to."

"To write poetry?"

"Oh, I make no claims to poetic talent."

"To catch herring, then?"

"No, not that either. I plan to take pictures there. I'm here waiting for plates from Reykjavik."

You've got it good, I thought.

"Come on in," I said.

Then the whole gang of us rushed into the packhouse and when we were all seated around on the floor Stefan began to tell us about his merry life as a photographer. He had traveled around in all parts of the country and taken pictures of many people and made them all pay half in advance. And people were so eager to have their picture taken that some of them had him make three exposures and paid half for each in advance. Then the photographer had repaired to his home to develop the pictures. The people out in the country were always looking forward to seeing the pictures and wondering how they would look. But then it began to be taking a rather long time for the development and it finally turned out that the photographer had overlooked to load the camera before he took the pictures. He earned quite a bit by this method. We were filled with envy and admiration.

"It's not necessary to be broke all the time," remarked Stefan, "if you just understand people well enough."

After Stefan joined our ranks our group took on a still more poetic hue. We wandered about the streets from morning to night in a lyrical daze and talked with great sensitivity about poetry and genius and recited verses and poems in trembling tones. It was during this period that Stefan wrote several of the poems that later, when they were published, were to place him in the foremost ranks of Icelandic poets through the ages.

But occasionally we fell from these poetic heights into the ugly reality of daily life, where we always were faced by the same dilemma. The herring had not yet arrived and showed no sympathy for the problems of unemployed men. We had even begun to lose all hope that we would ever be shown any mercy that summer. And our relationship to the Post Office was by this time anything but lyrical.

But just about this time the news came that the herring had entered Eyjafjord, just a short ways to the east. A longing to reach Akureyri, the largest town in Eyjafjord, flamed up in us, but since we were all broke there seemed little hope that it would ever be satisfied. At this point Stefan showed his true worth and secured for us all free passage on a boat to Akureyri. What a man!

The sun set slowly behind the western mountains on that last lyrical day.

Akureyri

IT WAS 11:30 A.M. on Monday the fifteenth of July when we departed from Siglufjord, without first having taken time to leave our thanks at the Post Office for all the food we had eaten there. It was cloudy and windy with occasional gusts of sharp rain. The waves ran high and the horizon was dark and foreboding.

Life now took on a different tone than it had had on the streets of Siglufjord. My companions became violently seasick and huddled only half conscious in some bare bunks down in the filthy, reeking cabin. They were no longer lyrical. I sat alone at the back of the cabin on a bench and worked myself up into a poetic-philosophic frenzy, sang old sea songs and racked my brain to figure out what happens to a man's soul when he becomes seasick.

Stefan went ashore in Hjalteyri while the rest of us continued on to Akureyri, where we arrived at eight o'clock in the evening. Thorleif, Gunnar, and I marched straight to the finest hotel in town. It was called Hotel Akureyri and lay at the foot of a hill a ways from the harbor. We had never before in our lives seen such rooms: large and bright, with red plush chairs and white-clad maids and windows looking out on the green slope of the hill. We took two adjoining rooms. Thorleif and Gunnar were to sleep in the double bed in one room and I was to have the other.

Then we went to bed. But we found each other so entertaining that we could not bring ourselves to part company. So we opened the doors between the two rooms and moved the beds over to them so that the headboards were together.

I began singing the praises of the carefree life of a poet and philosopher but was interrupted by Thorleif who snarled in an unpleasant, teasing tone of voice:

"That's just like you!"

"What do you mean it's like me?"

"You just wander around and never settle down and do an honest day's work."

"I don't understand."

"That's all right. He'll understand tomorrow morning when he has to pay for the room," Gunnar interjected.

"Yes, what are you going to pay with, anyway?"

"That's none of your business."

"Well, well, that's strange if it's none of our business. If you can't pay, then Gunnar and I'll get stuck for it all."

"I cover my own debts."

"What the hell are you going to cover them with, you lazy little broke bastard? What are you going to pay with, anyway?"

"With money, of course."

"What money?"

"I'm not in the least bit inclined to give you an accounting for such things here. Besides that, you're incapable of understanding the way a poet thinks. What do you know about poetry? You don't even know an iamb from a trochee."

"You're a damn fool. To give up a good job working on the road to wander out into the unknown. Is that supposed to be poetry? Do you think you can pay for your room with iambs and trochees?"

"My God! What an imbecile. To eat at the Post Office for a crown a day and not have the guts to get a job for the summer. It'll be fun to see how you get back to Reykjavik! Maybe he thinks he can trochee his way to Reykjavik! Or sail on that little tub of a sweetheart of his in Hrutafjord!"

"Oh no. He'll never get up enough courage to climb aboard her. I've never before known such an idiot. It's no wonder you write poems about your miserable and wretched life."

"Let's just let them throw him in jail if he's not able to pay for his room before tomorrow at sundown."

I sorely repented that I had ever broached this explosive subject. I rose early the next morning, dressed angrily, grabbed my walking-stick and let it whistle over the heads of those two devils:

"I'll never speak to you again, never as long as I live. You're the most unpoetic swine I've ever known. You don't understand a poet's soul. You have no conception of the sufferings of a genius. You don't know a thing about poetry. Even a cat understands more about art than you."

Then I hurried out of the hotel and combed the town for a job.

I hadn't been looking long before I realized what a spot I was in. I couldn't get anything to do anywhere although I ran moaning from one employer to another. I didn't have a penny for food or a crown for a roof over my head. I went hungry all day long and felt ashamed to be alive. This was the world of stark reality. After futile visits to every pier on the harbor I wandered far out of town and hid my misery among the hillocks, drew a razor-sharp pocket knife out of my jacket pocket and lay it open beside me in case I did not succeed in making myself forget this sorrowful world's daily bread.

Toward evening I stuck the knife back in my pocket and staggered weakly back toward town. Then I heard that Stefan had come to town for the evening and that a little party was being thrown at Hotel Oddeyri. I headed in that direction. After a few drinks all the cares of life had evaporated. The world once more smiled upon me with promises of plenty of work and good pay. And what a world!

The next day I got a job working in the herring on one of the piers.

Tryggvi from Eyjafjord

IT WAS eleven o'clock and I had just finished my first arduous day on the pier. I was dirty, wet and exhausted. I was quivering from fatigue and longed for sleep and rest but I hadn't had time to look for a room, nor could I think of any lodgings for the night that I could afford.

I was standing at a loss for what to do beside a pile of barrels at the end of the pier when a young man came over to me. On his head he had the crownless remains of a hat which he lifted in solemn silence. Then he spoke to me in a gentle, courteous tone of voice:

"You can stay with me until you have found lodgings. I have a room in the school up on the hill there."

As he talked he raised his right hand and pointed at a large wooden building on the top of a high, steep hill a little ways above the main street that ran through the whole town parallel to the fjord.

The wave of gratitude that swept through me almost brought on a heart attack. This man must have read "Night" and was one of those who don't like to see geniuses suffer. We plodded along the winding road up the hill and discussed Hamlet.

This good young man was named Tryggvi Sveinbjarnarson and was a student and a poet. He was from Eyjafjord and in Reykjavik was always referred to as Tryggvi from Eyjafjord. He was of medium height, well-built and exceedingly masculine. His hair was light, his eyes gray and his features handsome. But what really distinguished his appearance was his extreme nearsightedness. This gave him a certain charm that people with normal eyesight lack. He always looked as if he was extremely interested in anything he was looking at. And it in addition afforded him the opportunity to use a lorgnette. This piece of equipment added such a touch of distinction to his appearance that some of us wished nothing more than to be just a little bit nearsighted so that we too could use lorgnettes. As a matter of fact, several of our group actually acquired gilded lorgnettes containing window glass that they raised to their eyes when they wanted to appear distinguished, especially if there were any young ladies watching.

Tryggvi was an unusually good-natured man. He was most often happy, congenial and helpful. His mind was entirely occupied with poetry, music and the mystery of beautiful women. He swam through life in a dramatic dreamworld, across a beautifully decorated stage where the curtain rose and fell in time with the romantic fluctuations of unexperienced youthful infatuation. He knew little about the practical things of life. Science, politics and philosophical pondering were foreign languages to him. He knew nothing about God and seemed to forget each day as soon as it had passed. He made only moderate use of alcohol, especially when he was treating.

It was Tryggvi's highest dream in those days to become a famous playwright, and it can't be denied that he had considerable talents in that direction. During the summer of 1912 he was working on a play which, he confided in us, the theater in Reykjavik would perform the following winter. This gained him a good deal of respect down at the pier. Nor was it any daily occurrence in Akureyri to see a playwright working in the herring—to work on a filthy herring pier with a poet who was always thinking thoughts that thousands of people later would see and admire and applaud until the author appeared on the stage in a tuxedo and bowed three times. A young girl in a white dress and with golden hair and blue eyes would walk onto the stage, blush and hand him a large bouquet of white and red roses. Some spectators in the back of the auditorium would call out:

"Bravo! Hurra! That was a hell of a fine play!"

And as those present at the première returned home they would remark among themselves:

"He is without a doubt the greatest writer in the history of Iceland."

It was also known to various people, both in Reykjavik and Akureyri, that Tryggvi had written a novel about a poor widow who owned a little house. Then, as the Fates would have it, the house caught fire. But the widow's love for her former husband was so much stronger than her love for the treasures of this world that she made no effort to save anything from the flames except the chair that her husband had sat in when he was alive. With a smile on her lips and her heart full of love she emerged from the flames carrying the chair and let everything else burn. That was true love that reached beyond the grave. This story of never-ending love made a deep impression on various young men who had subscribed to the increasingly popular moral dogma of that day that love disappears as the sexual glands age.

Tryggvi and I worked on the same pier that summer.

He was a good worker although, to be sure, a bit erratic. When the spirit was on him he could work like a fiend and since he was so popular because of his poetic gifts the bosses tended to overlook it that he sometimes did almost nothing.

It was his custom to climb up on a herring barrel in the evening before work was finished and hold a bellowing speech, usually spiced with various strange sounds. All hands on the pier stopped their work, all activity ceased, not a sound was heard, people leaned out of the windows of the houses beside the pier and everyone stared at the speaker and listened with such attention that it bordered on worship. The subject matter and form of expression of these speeches were so unlike all worldly matters that it was practically impossible to review their true contents afterwards. But there was hardly any question that such wisdom had never before been heard on the pier. Tryggvi was indisputably the most original and talented man among us that summer. And no one could approach his personal popularity with the other workers.

Tryggvi had lodgings in a classroom at the north end of the school. It happened one evening when we were home that he asked me to slip down to the south end of the hall and see if there was a woman's hat and coat hanging there on a hook. I trotted off to the south end of the hall, investigated each and every coat hook, returned to our room and said that no woman's hat or coat was to be found on any hook. A dark shadow fell over my friend's face upon hearing this.

I stared at him.

"What's the matter? Is it the hat and coat? You aren't by chance in love, my friend?"

"Yes, I'm in love."

"Well, well, you're not alone in that. Why haven't you told me before this?"

"It's a secret."

"A secret! Don't be a fool. Does she live here at the school?"

"Yes, upstairs at the south end."

"Then perhaps it's the schoolmaster's maid."

"It's his daughter, Hulda."

"Oh-ho! Not bad. You don't set your sights low. Do you love her very much?"

"I'll never live another happy day if I don't get her."

"Does she love you?"

"That's just what I don't know."

"Have you ever kissed her?"

"No, not yet. I've only once touched her coat."

"That's not much. But why did you ask me to check her hat and coat? Isn't she true to you?"

"She sometimes goes out in the evening."

"Maybe there's someone else who's also in love with her."

"That's precisely what I'm afraid of. I've got a suspicion that there's another fellow trying to get hold of her and that's why it's so hellish when her hat and coat are gone in the evening."

"I can understand that well, Tryggvi. I've also always considered it to be very suspicious when girls have been on the go in the evening. I knew one who took off with a pile of music under her arm at nine o'clock each Wednesday and Sunday evening and claimed to be going to an organ lesson. But I've always wondered just what sort of organ lesson it was."

"Did you ever find out if the teacher was a man?"

"Yes. It was some dope from up north here. I doubt if he knew anything about music at all."

"I suspect it wasn't necessary either. I once knew a girl from out west who received tutoring in Danish each Thursday evening at nine o'clock."

"And didn't learn very much?"

"She learned what she went to learn."

"Oh, my God! Are they all like that? I suspect that the girl I was talking about learned very little about playing the organ. I never heard her sing more than two songs all winter long, always the same two songs, and she knew them both before she began to take organ lessons. I've always been afraid that this business about organ lessons and being tutored in Danish was just a cover-up for something else. Now I'll tell you the truth about all this. I'm gradually becoming more and more convinced that all girls who find an excuse to go out in the evening are nothing but man-hungry even though they're not supposed to have such inclinations until they're married. Therefore you should take care to let them know, if you're in love with them, that they don't have to go out to get it. Otherwise their instincts will drive them to mysterious teachers and tutors who rob you of peace of mind and sleep, disrupt your work and tear your soul to shreds, because girls find no satisfaction in turning away anyone coming with an offer of honorable marriage. They all live in and for the moment. And they in reality can't help themselves. They're just made that way. That's what I've heard, anyway. So take my advice and let her understand that that which she seeks in other houses can also be found in this house."

"But she's not like that, Thorbergur."
"Doesn't she have rosy cheeks?"
"No. She's pale."
"Well, then maybe she's not so dangerous for you. The red ones are the most dangerous, since they have the warmest blood. The one who took organ lessons was dark red. How about the one who took Danish lessons?"

"Crimson to the roots of her hair. And plump and juicy."

"Then she wasn't without the proper instincts. Wasn't she just wild?"

"I don't know. I never gave her Danish lessons."
"Is Hulda the first girl you've been in love with?"
"No. And this is really only the result of despair."
"What? Despair? Has some girl let you down?"
"No. But I was in love with another girl whom I can never forget. I'm positive I'll love her as long as I live. I'll probably be unhappy the rest of my life because of her."

"Well, then you're in the same fix as I. What's her name?"

"You must never tell anyone. Her name is Catherine Nordmann."

"Ah! A gorgeous girl. I saw her once last spring and I was told that her name was Catherine Nordmann. I wasn't so fond of the girl I was in love with the rest of the evening."

"She's the most beautiful girl in the world."
"Did she love you?"
"She never said. She never said anything."
"Did you ever get to kiss her?"
"No, I never even got an arm around her."
"Didn't you ever ask her for a kiss?"

"No. I never dared. That's just what made my love stronger and more lasting."

"Do you think that love fades when you kiss them?"

"Yes. That love burns hottest, that never kisses, Shakespeare says some place."

"Did you love her an awful lot?"

"What do you mean by 'an awful lot'?"

"So that you, for example, would be willing to die for her."

"I couldn't think of any greater joy than to be crucified for her with my head down."

"My God! Really?"

"I swear it's the truth. I loved her so terribly much that everything she touched became transformed for me into an image of herself. I sneaked up to the door of her house in the evening just so that I could touch the door handle she had touched during the day. And then I kissed the handle as I stepped back from the door and whispered 'Good night'. Once I got her to play the piano for me. The window to her room was open and I stood with my head uncovered on the street below the window while she played."

"I've never loved so deeply as that. And she still didn't repay your love?"

"Yes. One time. Only one time."

"But yet you never got to kiss her. What did you get?"

"It happened like this: one bright, moonlit night we were skating together when we both fell and slid down a little slope, breast to breast, in such a way that I saw straight into her lovely deep blue eyes that shone in the moonlight. That was the most glorious moment I have ever lived and I prayed with tears in my eyes, as we slid down the slope, that our whole life might be thus."

"And that was all?"

"Yes, I wasn't destined to receive more. But in these few moments was concentrated more happiness than in all the other moments of my life combined. In the fraction of a minute that we slid breast to breast down the slope my love attained such deep satisfaction that I didn't kiss her door handle for several days."

"That's the greatest love I've ever heard of. And it is all over between you?"

"All over! Far from it. It will never be over! Now she's living in Reykjavik."

"Haven't you met her there?"

"Yes, once."

"Didn't you try to get even a kiss then?"

"No. It was Christmas Eve last winter. I found my way to the house where she lives with mother and brothers and sisters. The wind was from the north and it was biting cold and I had neither overcoat nor gloves. The light of Christmas candles streamed out of the windows of her house. I had no candles in my room. After I had been standing a while outside her house I saw her pass in front of the window. What do you think I did then?"

"You didn't begin to sing 'O, little town of Bethlehem'?"

"I grabbed an icicle hanging from her house and threw it up at the window to let her know that I was outside and that I intended to keep Christmas out there on the street in front of her house. I was delighted to be so near her. I felt beautiful and gentle rays stream through me when I stroked with my bare hand the ice-cold corrugated iron that covered her house and shielded her body from the wind. And thus I celebrated Christmas Eve until long past midnight, coatless, gloveless, in the cold winter storm."

"Didn't you freeze, Tryggvi? Weren't you afraid of getting pneumonia?"

"No, my friend. I didn't feel the cold at all until I had started home and the Christmas lights from her windows disappeared around the corner."

I sat and listened to him in speechless amazement. He's crazy, nutty, he's stark raving mad, I muttered to myself. And he calls that having met her once!

One hot, sunny day later on in the summer things were exceptionally busy down at the pier. Two ships had just arrived, loaded with herring, and the entire cargo was on the point of spoiling due to the heat. All hands worked like mad to save the catch, unloading, cleaning, salting and barreling the fish, sweating and swearing and running about.

Just when the tempo reached its most frenzied we saw Tryggvi suddenly stop work and stare as if hypnotized in the direction of the school. Then his body was seized by sharp convulsions. He grabbed a barrel-head that was lying on an empty barrel, pulled a pencil out of his pocket and began scribbling something on the barrel-head.

It didn't take me long to figure out what was going on. It was the spirit itself that, right in the middle of the day's toil, had chosen my room-mate to be the bearer of some stirring message to this slaving, materialistic world. It had come to me just like that on that wonderful night on High Street when it chose me to reveal "Night" to all people.

I went over to Tryggvi and said to him quietly, reverently:

"Did you receive an inspiration?"

He made no answer, but lifted the barrel-head up to

his eyes and passionately read what he had written, so loudly that it could be heard from one end of the pier to the other:

"Hulda, sweetest Hulda,
my rosebud fair and bright!
Hulda, dearest Hulda,
most precious heavenly light!

I'll remember thee, o maid,
while the golden breakers roar,
while the rushing waves cascade
in exultation on the shore.

Hulda, gentle Hulda,
my heart belongs to thee.
Hulda, gentle Hulda,
do come and be with me."

That evening he took the barrel-head home with him and hung it up on the wall over his bed.

Romantic Days

THE SOLEMN nocturnal conversations that Tryggvi and I indulged in about the trials and tribulations of young lovers, the inscrutability of the female soul and other such subjects weighing on our minds were suddenly and without warning terminated. I found myself one day standing at the window of a red house surveying the tiny patch of the endless expanse of the universe that was to be the object of my soul's contemplation during the next two months.

This window was located in the room which Gunnar had rented upstairs in the Akureyri branch of the Bank of Iceland. It faced south, was twelve by eight and about a third of this area was under the slope of the roof. It opened onto a broad hallway that resembled a drying attic.

I had suddenly moved into this room with all my belongings: my books and papers, pens and ink, astronomical charts, pipes and tobacco; separated from my best friend, the most pure-hearted and unhappiest lover in the world, only three short days after I had first met him on the pier.

Gunnar had rented the room with the intention that we would live there together and that Thorleif, who had been working at a small town a ways up the fjord, would have a place to stay if he found anything to do in Akureyri. Just a few days after I had moved in he arrived and we were three in the room the rest of the summer.

August arrived. Day after day the cold autumn rain swept in from the north and the surrounding mountain slopes were half covered with snow. On the pier we slopped around in rain and snow and herring under the eternal gray sky. Soaked to the skin, aching and groggy we dragged ourselves home from work in pitch darkness after twelve to twenty hours of the struggle for existence. This was civilization! I will love my native land . . .

Then one murky, depressing evening a bit of unexpected news lit up the darkness on the pier: Stefan from Whitedale had arrived in town and was living at Hotel Oddeyri!

Bravo!

The next day we heard that he had photographed a lot of people up north and that they all had paid half in advance. He had told the servants at the hotel that he would be extremely busy next few weeks and needed a quiet room where he could develop his pictures. This news was whispered from man to man as if it were top-secret information. And for several days Stefan never left his room unless he had his camera with him. There could be no doubt about it. This was a serious and hard-working photographer.

But it was also whispered about that he had had to leave his bags behind in one of the towns up north. A committee of young and determined men was formed at Hotel Oddeyri to institute action to recover them for him. How come he had to leave his bags behind? This was the question of the day on the herring piers.

As it turned out, however, Stefan did not overexert himself developing pictures. He immediately joined our ranks and took an energetic part in our poetic activity. Once more we experienced bright, dream-filled days. In the evening after work we dressed in our finest and wandered about the streets of the town and let our lyrical natures pour forth, either extolling the joys of existence or lamenting the tragedy of a ruined life.

One lush August evening there was a dance at the Masonic Temple. We dressed ourselves to kill and joined the crowd, but we only stood by and watched. Our faces shone with respectability as we virtuously strode past bulging blouses and tempting, sweeping skirts that spoke the most beautiful language in the world. We're not the kind of fellows who deceive innocent little girls who are now dozing safely amidst the fragrant glory of the mountains of chastity!

On Sundays we often took riding trips or boisterously drove around in colorful fancy carriages, always drunk, always infatuated, always either deliriously happy or eternally doomed. And in the evenings we all sat around and feasted at the hotel, declaiming, disputing, singing, reciting.

Gunnar sang heart-rending songs about lovers who were parted by a cruel fate and never reunited. He sang about a lovely girl who waited day after day for her beloved and spun the while. And she spun and she spun and she spun, but her beloved never came. Why didn't he ever come? And he sang about a maiden with rosy cheeks who stood alone at the foot of a high mountain. She constantly gazed upwards at the mountain because she longed so much to cross it, but there were incessant storms on the mountain and so she never crossed it, never, never.

Why were there always storms on the mountain? Why did she want to cross the mountain? We listened with tears in our eyes. The hotel guests rewarded Gunnar with free beer.

One day we threw a big party at the hotel in honor of Stefan and his contribution to the struggle for existence. The immediately preceding days were days of hectic preparation for the participants. I stayed up all one night composing a poem dedicated to Stefan. The first thing that my comrades caught sight of when they got up to go to work in the morning was me rocking back and forth on the couch with pen and ink in hand and surrounded by reams of white paper, mumbling some incomprehensible nonsense, wheezing and grinning like an idiot. They stared in astonishment at this mad creature who stayed awake all night thinking up some stupid poem and who then would be asleep on his feet at work all day long. What an incorrigible fool!

This great poem was about a young man who left his forefathers' farm and enthusiastically set off to climb the highest mountain in the world and from there reach the moon. He wanders at great length until he is tormented by hunger, exhaustion, bloodthirsty wolves, spooks and ghosts that leap out at him from creepy cracks and crevices on all sides. He loses his way and staggers about confused and desperate. The moon is eclipsed. The young man is seized by fear and when he stumbles against a chimney he climbs it in deadly terror, thinking that he is ascending the mountain. Enveloped by the thick clouds of billowing smoke from the chimney (symbolizing the clouded condition of his mind) he raises his voice and praises merciful God for his victory over the mountain. It was an old and tragic story.

A little past noon on Sunday the first of September the banquet began. Those were marvelous hours. The tables were covered with all forms and shapes of glasses, breakers, jiggers and tumblers. We crowded around the guest of honor, some of us reeking so strongly of herring that the others almost had to flee the room and break up the party. But by concentrating on spiritual matters we forgot the stench. Soon we were in high spirits and I leapt onto a chair, called for silence and began to declaim my poem. Each time I came to the refrain I flailed the back of the chair with my walking stick in time with the meter to pound it into the ears of my listeners and divert their attention all the more from their nostrils.

When I had finished I was met by a roar of applause and in great satisfaction I sat down and stole a look around. Yes, indeed, it was clear enough. My poem had been a great success. All the others were staring at me. This young man must be a great poet, probably a genius.

When the party was over a sleek horse hitched to a luxurious carriage stood before the hotel door. Beside the horse waited a courteous driver, slightly tipsy. He showed the geniuses of the day, Stefan and me, to seats in the carriage. Then we three drove out along the fjord until we got stuck in the sand after nearly having dumped the contents of the carriage in the river. We returned to the hotel and spent the evening quarreling about poetry.

Then we broke into tears.

Dead Days

How quickly time passed! Suddenly autumn had arrived, with its pale sunshine during the day and frost at night. The shadows of the houses reached farther and farther out into the street. A deep peace fell over the face of the earth and each evening more and more stars appeared in the heavens. Yesterday evening I saw Vindemiatrix for the first time.

The boats had ceased fishing. Some had sailed home to quivering sweethearts in idyllic fjords behind the mountains, others bobbed lonesomely at anchor out in the harbor. Fewer and fewer attended our get-togethers at Hotel Oddeyri and they gradually quieted down. Some of our most exuberant companions had already departed, and others were about to leave.

And I had once more begun to think of my beloved. For almost three months I had been wandering on the treacherous pathways of life and she had almost disappeared in the brilliance of these glorious days. But suddenly I saw her standing at the back door of my heart, as cheering and forbearing as an angel that always waits for the straying sheep at the end of the road, no matter how far the enticements of the tempter has led it from the way of the Lord. I invited her in. Please, do come in. We're alone. No one else ever enters here.

Do you realize that I've been waiting at this door for eleven whole weeks, dearest friend?

No, I didn't. I always left by the other door.

I didn't dare come that way. And I didn't want to knock. I was afraid I might bother you—you've had so much to do.

Yes, I've had a lot to do. I've sometimes had to work around the clock.

Yes, I know. But now this yoke is lifted from your shoulders. And autumn has come with its dusk that creeps into your blood and nerves and brings with it all those strange feelings and desires. You understand me.

Yes, I understand you. How good it was of you to wait for me all this time, my dearest. You haven't been out of my thoughts an instant since we parted. Do you know that I love you?

How do you love me?

I love you as one loves an angel.

She shook her head.

Why do you shake your head?

Because I am no angel.

I thought that all your thoughts were pure and without sin, as the thoughts of an angel.

She looked down as if she were overwhelmed by great fatigue.

My darling angel, I said to myself. I understand. You have grown tired of waiting.

After this meeting with my beloved I began to consider how I could best return to Reykjavik. Obviously the quickest would be to travel all the way by boat. That would take hardly more than two or three days. But the shortest paths are not always the most fun.

I had begun to burn with longing to see my beloved

again. And I also longed to see the fjord that gave her tongue its shimmering tones and her eyes their brilliant sparkle. I knew for sure that she and I would meet once more in Reykjavik around the middle of October. And that in all probability we would live in the same house during the winter. But it was such an eternity until then! And she couldn't bring the fjord to Reykjavik.

My soul had been in a state of great conflict recently. It had been the scene of a great struggle between her and the fjord, and I was the spoils. The most disturbing thing about the whole situation was that the fjord seemed to be gaining the upper hand as the summer passed. During the last few weeks I had even experienced moments when I felt that some part of my ego was contemplating the fjord as an independent work of art, without any woman in the picture at all. And this part of me longed to come into physical contact with this distant region which my beloved had made into the greatest work of art on earth. Last spring the fjord had only served as a background for her. Now she sometimes disappeared from the foreground without leaving a trace after herself on the ground or in the grass. She had given the fjord its beauty. Was the fjord now about to steal my love from her? Was she then the ephemeral? And the fjord the eternal?

In consternation I handed myself over to the unknown quantity behind the mist of worldly knowledge:

Am I more in love with the girl or with the fjord?

And the voice of the unknown answered from behind the mist of worldly knowledge:

The male within you is more in love with the girl. But the poet with the fjord. Last spring they both loved the girl more. Remember the wisdom of the eternal: Love the girl as you love the fjord. Love the fjord as you love the girl.

Then the male within me shouted: The poet must die!

So one day I went down to the steamship office and inquired about all possible boat connections with Hrutafjord. And fortunately for me a boat would arrive in Akureyri on the twenty-fourth of September and leave for Hrutafjord the next day and make only two stops on the way.

In a moment of inspiration I decided not to take the boat all the way to Hrutafjord, but only to Hvammstang, one of the two stops, and from there trace my steps back across the mountain to Hrutafjord and then to Borgarnes. This plan presented one problem, however. This route would take me along only the eastern shore of Hrutafjord and I was certain that my beloved would not be staying at any farm on the eastern shore. But there was a slight chance that she would be somewhere at the inner arm of the fjord, although in all probability she would be at a farm on the western shore at least fifteen miles off my route.

What was I to do?

Should I trudge up half the western shore of Hrutafjord in plain sight of everyone, asking as I went: Could you please tell me what farm my beloved is staying at now?

And when I had finally found her and dropped shyly and wearily at her feet, she would say: You'll really get me a fine reputation, letting half the county see you coming to find me in bright daylight. I'm no cheap pick-up.

And she would be entirely right. That would be a shocking impudence on my part. Such behavior could ruin a good girl's reputation, and it might even destroy her faith in my innocence. It would only serve to convince her that I was in reality nothing but a disgusting lecher. Just look: that's love. That's the man who thought he was above carnal desire. And it might convert her love for me into undying loathing.

This was really a tough problem. I could find no better way to solve it than simply to forget all about those fifteen miles from my route to my pure-hearted beloved. Don't worry about it for the time being. Something will turn up when the time comes.

In all other respects my journey was clear to me. Two days by boat to Hvammstang, then a day's hike to Hrutafjord. One or two days there with my beloved. Three days' hike from Hrutafjord to Borgarnes and from there to Reykjavik with the mailboat *Ingolfur*. Nine days at most. That wasn't much of a sacrifice for one's beloved in those days even though I could expect to have to slosh through the fall rains and floods on the way to Borgarnes. But what would that be in comparison with all the suffering she must have undergone since we last parted?

The next day I went to a tailor and ordered a new suit sewn. It would be a beautiful suit: light gray with dark gray pin stripes, cut in the latest style. No one would laugh at that suit. Then I bought a pair of new shoes and a wide-brimmed gray hat.

Thus clad I would appear before my beloved in Hrutafjord.

Fruitful Nights

THORLEIF and Gunnar left for home on the eleventh of September. I was now alone in the room and could undisturbed make astronomical observations and carry on nocturnal monologues about the ephemeral and the eternal without anyone eavesdropping on my thoughts. But shortly before I left for Reykjavik it so happened that Stefan from Whitedale found himself without a place to stay, and he shared the room with me the last nights I was in Akureyri.

I don't believe I'll ever forget those nights. We shared the big bed Thorleif and Gunnar had slept in before and he told me about his amazingly varied experiences in life until the wee hours of the morning. His fascinating accounts in the attentive September nights stroked a rusty string in my breast and restored its tone.

One evening I told Stefan about my intention to take the boat to Hvammstang and then hike to Hrutafjord to see my beloved.

"Have you ever loved so much that you could have set off on such a journey just to be able to talk to your beloved a couple of hours?" I asked.

"Yes; God knows I have," he replied. "It's not much more than a year ago that a girl died that I could have walked from one end of the country to the other for."

"And is she dead now?"

"Yes, she died in May last year."

"Did you miss her much after she was dead?"

"I'll never be the same man. The wounds from pure young love never heal."

"Was she your first love?"

"Yes, my first pure love."

"Do you think it's impossible for a man to forget the first girl he loved?"

"That depends on how he loved her."

"What? Is there more than one way to love?"

"If love is pure and deep, you never recover from it."

"But how can you tell if your love is pure and deep?"

"Love is always pure and deep if you have no desire to sleep with the girl."

"Is then love never pure and deep if you desire that?"

"No, love is then never from God."

"But now let's say that the girl won't marry you. Should you then try to sleep with her so as not to be destroyed by love? Does that help any?"

"Yes, that helps. If you sleep with the girl you get over it quickly. And you should always be sure to do that if a girl won't have you."

"But don't you lose her completely then? Doesn't that disgust her?"

"No. They always want more. Are you such a child?"

"I know an old man who lost his wife after many years of living with her and it went so far between them that they even had children. But yet he was so affected by his wife's death that he has been drowning his sorrows in drink ever since. It doesn't look like he'll ever get over it."

"Well, maybe. But how about you? Haven't you ever gotten anything from that girl out in Hrutafjord that you're in love with?"

"No. I swear by God that I've never so much as kissed her."

"Haven't you ever wanted to?"

"Yes, a little bit sometimes. But I've never dared try anything like that. I've been afraid that she'd think I was fresh. We are bound together by purely spiritual love."

"Such nonsense doesn't exist except between sexless preadolescents. There's no such thing as love until you've been to bed with the girl."

"But you just said that you had no desire to sleep with a girl if your love for her is pure and deep. What should I believe?"

"Oh, did I say that? Well, don't worry, just believe what I'm telling you now. Haven't you ever been able to see that she wanted you to make a pass at her?"

"Well, I don't know quite what to say to that. Sometimes I've thought I could, sometimes not. It's not easy to see through these women."

"Didn't you ever notice that she trembled when you were with her?"

I felt as if I had been stabbed in the heart. I tried desperately to keep my voice from cracking as I answered after a short pause:

"Well, not precisely. But one night when we were standing in front of her door she suddenly told me that she was trembling all over."

"And what did you do then?"

"Nothing. I just said that she should hurry to get to bed and get warm."

"My God! What a fool you are!"

"Why am I a fool?"

"Don't you know why girls tremble like that?"

"Because they want to be touched a bit?" burst out of me as I tossed in the bed and broke out in a cold sweat.

"Yes, of course. That's a sure sign. Didn't you know that that trembling comes from sexual hunger?"

"No; I swear I didn't. How should I have?"

"Just what did you think she meant by it?"

"I thought maybe she was getting pneumonia and let her go right to bed so she could get warm."

"You're the biggest idiot about women that I've ever run into, even if you are gifted and a fine poet. Ha-ha-ha-ha-ha-ha-hah! I've never heard anything like it."

"What should I have done? It was pitch dark."

"You need light for it? You should have put your arm around the girl and pulled her close up to you and told her that you love her. And then you should have taken her into her room and sat on the edge of the bed with her as a beginning."

"But what if she had become angry and threatened to complain to the landlord about me?"

"If she had gotten cantankerous you should have stroked her neck."

"Is that good?"

"Women can't resist it. Then they just fall right into your arms. You can get any girl you want just by stroking her neck properly."

"Do you think I should try to stroke her neck when I meet her now in Hrutafjord?"

"You can try. But I really doubt if it will do any good. If she's like other women, then I'm afraid she has only contempt for you now."

"Why should she have contempt for me. I've always been polite to her."

"That's not being polite. That's being a fool. Hot-blooded girls always have contempt for men who don't let anything happen. They think they're impotent."

"Oh. Well, what should I do to set this right. Maybe I shouldn't try to stroke her neck after all. What are you mumbling about?"

"I'm saying my prayers."

"What. Do you still say your prayers in the evening?"

"Of course. I always pray to God before I go to sleep. Don't speak to me for a while . . .

"It's not so easy to set right if she's contemptuous of you. You could try stroking her. And then you should caress her breasts a little and tell her you love her. Does she have nice breasts? . . .

"The Lord make his face to shine upon me and give me peace. Amen . . .

"Does she have nice breasts? But you mustn't do it in front of anyone else. Just when you're alone with her, behind a locked door."

"Do you think I'm dumb enough to let others see it?! But what if that doesn't do it? What then?"

"O-o-o-oh, I'm tired. What were you saying?"

"I asked, what should I do if that doesn't work?"

"Then tell her you're in love with someone else. O-o-o-o-oh-ho-o-o-o-o. What was that? Did the alarm ring? Z-z-z-z-z-z-z-z-u-u-u-u-u-u-u-u-uh."

It was the middle of the night. This giant of wisdom in the ways of life was now peaceably snoring and grunting. I lay awake a long time, my heart pounding, my nerves taut. I tossed and turned, plagued by the most piercing pangs of conscience. What a fool I'd been! What an idiot!

I lay awake the whole night trying to find a way to make right my transgression against this lovely girl who had borne such great suffering all winter long with such equilibrium that she had never complained, never grumbled, and only once whispered softly: I'm trembling all over.

On the Move

WEDNESDAY the twenty-fifth of September dawned clear and bright. The sun was shining and there was not a breath of wind. Smoke rose straight up from chimneys on all sides and the houses and hills of Akureyri were reflected in the glassy fjord. An occasional sleepy footstep was borne up to me in the stillness of the morning from the street below. I never heard those footsteps again.

I got up early, collected my belongings and stuffed them into my bags and locked them securely. Having done this I sat down on one of the bags and regarded my bed-fellow, the wisest man I had yet met in my wanderings through life. He was awake and was half lying in bed, apparently unaware of my presence. He was humming and staring at the wall at the foot of the bed.

"Well, my friend," I said, almost with tears in my voice, "now we must part. And God knows if we'll ever meet again in this life, or in all eternity."

Then my friend turned his head in my direction, looked at me and said.

"I am quite positive that we'll meet again."

"Have you dreamed about it?"

"Yes, I had a dream in which it was revealed to me that we will meet again, although I don't know when. And we will both live to a ripe old age. You will become a great philosopher and I will become a famous poet."

"Well, well, let's hope so. But before we part now I'd like to return to the last question I asked you last night. To be sure, you answered it then, but I'm not sure that you had considered your answer carefully enough. You were half asleep."

"Was it about that girl you're in love with?"

"Yes. I asked you what I should do if she didn't soften up when I stroked her and you answered that I then should tell her that I was in love with another. Do you think that's wise? Tell me the truth now."

"Oh, my God, no! Never do that. Then she'd think you were a complete idiot—to be in love with two girls at once. Don't you see that? But you should let her know that there's a young and beautiful girl right next door who's wild to marry you."

"But what if she should say: All right. So long. That's fine by me. Then I'd be in a nice mess."

"You can rest assured that she'd never say that. You're the kind of fellow that once a girl has been in love with you, she'll never want to let you go."

"But if that's the case do I really need to lie to her about someone else wanting to marry me?"

"Of course. It'll do her good to hear it. Are you such a fool? Does she have nice breasts?"

"I don't know."

"Haven't you ever seen them?"

"Are you crazy?!"

"Haven't you ever played with them?"

"God forgive you!"

"Does her blouse bulge out much?"

"I've never noticed."

"Haven't you ever looked at her?"

"Yes, but never there. Do you think it's really safe to do what you've told me to?"

"Yes, yes. There's no danger. I know much more about this than you do."

"Well, my friend, it's almost time for the boat to leave. I've got to hurry. Goodbye, and I hope things go as you wish them to."

"Goodbye. I'll drop you a line sometime this winter if I'm still above ground. Will you write to me, too?"

"Yes, I promise I will."

Then I went to the door, opened it, turned on the threshold and looked back at the great philosopher half lying on the bed and tried to fasten his image upon my memory so that I could later use it as a guiding light through the murky darkness of uncertain life. The last words I heard from his lips, just as the door closed between us, were:

"Write and tell me when you've been to bed with her, and let me know how it went."

He always had his wits about him.

Then I ran down the stairs and out onto the street, dressed in my new clothes and carrying a walking stick in my hand. Over my left arm I carried a shiny black raincoat wrapped around my work shoes. Right in front of the house I met the landlord, the bank director himself. I tipped my hat and said:

"I was just on my way to you to pay what I owe you."

I reached into my pocket and handed him the money. He took it, looked at it and said:

"You owe me more than that."

"How can that be? I thought that was all I owed you of my part of the rent."

"That's right. But your companions didn't pay up when they left."

"Oh? Didn't they pay up? I'd gladly pay their share if I could."

"You all went in on the room together, so you'll have to pay what they owe."

"I can hardly see that it's fair to ask me to pay others' debts, especially as things are now for me. I would have been glad to pay if I'd been a little better off, but now I'm almost broke. I'll be lucky to get home to Reykjavik."

"That doesn't concern me. If you don't pay up right away I'll get a lawyer after you as soon as you get to Reykjavik."

I felt as if a wire carding brush were being scraped along my spine when I heard the bank director say the word "lawyer." Lawyers were for me not human beings. They were learned hyenas whom the forces of evil sicked on poor, innocent people to cheat them and throw them in prison.

I fumbled, terror-stricken, in my pocket and gave the bank director the rest of the rent. I had only a little over twelve crowns left to get all the way to Reykjavik!

I ran down to the dock and jumped aboard the boat just as it was pulling away from shore. I found a quiet spot to stand and sent a look full of longing and mourning back at the town as the ship slowly gathered speed and sailed out of the fjord. In this romantic little fishing town which the ship was with increasing speed reducing to a memory I had seen my life shortened by seventy days. Today I am seventy-one days older than I was the day that I stepped ashore here, seventy-one days nearer death, the grave and judgment. The hairs of my head have become fewer, the furrows in my brow deeper and the circulation of my blood slower.

I removed my hat and my soul cried out:

"Farewell, Akureyri! Farewell, Hotel Oddeyri! Peace be with you, oh lovely little hillside, oh tufted fields that harbor lovers' moonlit trysts! Peace be with you, oh little houses with little people with little incomes and a little god on a little throne in a little heaven! Peace be with you, oh transient summer, oh withering blossoms, oh sighing grass! Peace be with you, oh inconstant life that fades like an intoxication and disappears irretrievably into the shadow of the inevitable! Peace be with you, oh dearest friend, oh Iceland's wisest man!"

I put my hat on and strolled along the deck looking for the second class cabins.

Oh, my God!! It would be difficult to describe how I felt when I suddenly saw an open hatchway yawning at me from where I expected to find the entrance to the second class cabins. I panicked and began to race desperately around the deck. Weren't the second class cabins supposed to be here? Or maybe here? Or over there?

No, the second class cabins seemed to have evaporated into thin air. In utter confusion I dashed up to one of the crewmen and breathlessly asked in my best Danish where I could find the second class cabins.

He calmly informed me that there no longer was second class on this boat. It had been converted into cargo room. This change had been made several years before when the ship had been taken out of regular coastal traffic. Now it sailed between Denmark and Iceland and only took occasional passengers at the Icelandic ports on its route.

I was ruined! I had only enough money for a second

class cabin without meals. A first class cabin with the required full board was out of the question.

I returned to the open hatchway and stared down into the hold. I hadn't been mistaken. Nothing but cargo down there. I beat my eyes with my fists: Why the hell can't you see second class cabins instead of that damned hold? I'll knock you out of my head if you insist on seeing that hold.

I couldn't spend the night down there. Dark as pitch. No place to lie. And my new clothes would have been ruined by the time I appeared before my beloved. That would have been enough to destroy her love for me. And I could then stroke her neck all I wanted to without avail. And I would have no chance of having any company down there. The only other passenger aboard was a girl on the way to a boarding school. And boarding school girls don't sleep in cargo rooms.

I wandered around on deck until evening came, distressed, desperate, despairing. Then in my desperation I sneaked down into the first class section and hid away in a lower bunk in a cabin farthest back in a corner. No sooner had I withdrawn to this dark retreat and the worst pangs of weariness had left me, than I realized more clearly than ever what a miserable plight I was in. There were only three possible ways for this all to end:

First, I would be held captive on the ship and taken to Copenhagen and there sentenced to hard labor and beaten and chained until I had worked off my debt. And what then? How would I be able to return home? I would be killed by Danish thieves or sold as a white slave to a whorehouse. Second, I would be turned over to the sheriff at the first port. He would place me in solitary confinement and put chains on me and whip me in the darkness bellowing:

So you thought you'd cheat the boat company, huh? Answer me, you dog. You thought you'd cheat the boat company, huh? Why don't you answer, you swindling little devil?

But the third possibility seemed most likely to me: I would be sworn at and sent ashore at Hvammstang and a lawyer in Reykjavik would be notified. As soon as I arrived in Reykjavik he would turn me over to the police. They in turn would bind me and drive me through the streets of town for all to see. The sidewalks would be crowded and the whole town would know of my crime. After a fitting time on bread and water I would be released and for the rest of my life everybody in town would point at me as I passed on the street and shout:

There he goes! The scoundrel who cheated the boat company and got six months on bread and water . . . There's that devil who got two years for swindling. Take a good look at him! Jailbird! Thief!

I trembled as I lay in the bunk. This was the first time in my life I had ever been dishonest in money matters and I was aflame with pangs of conscience. I didn't dare move a muscle and hardly drew a breath for fear that someone might find me. I stared into the darkness and listened to the sounds around me. Everything around me was strangely, remarkably loaded with hate. The creaking of the screw, the rolling of the ship, the shadows' shifting form on the wall, the cold beam of light that came in through the skylight above the door—this all closed around me like a foreign world, an enemy land that I hated and that hated me.

Although I searched to the limits of my consciousness I could nowhere discover the dimmest ray of hope, the slightest consolation. But suddenly I saw my beloved drift forth from the darkness, beautiful and inspiring. She smiled at me and said:

Please stop torturing your conscience about the money for your ticket. If the purser asks you to pay before you get to Hvammstang, you just tell him you'll pay when you get to Hvammstang. And when you get to Hvammstang, just sneak ashore without paying a penny. Won't you offer even that much for me? I've been waiting for you for twelve weeks now. I'm trembling all over.

Yes, my love. I'll try. I'd do anything for you, my angel.

Then she was gone, leaving behind only a tiny swirl of light and warmth that wrapped itself around me and led me into the realm of dreamless sleep.

The next day I lay still as a mouse, hidden in the shadow of the upper bunk. No one appeared looking for me, and that was good. I had begun to hope that everybody had forgotten about me, or that no one had noticed me when I sneaked into the cabin, and that I would be able to follow my beloved's advice.

But about four o'clock in the afternoon I heard heavy steps in the hallway outside. They stopped at my door and a knock came. Everything inside me stopped working. The enemy had come to demand my fare! I'll pay when I get to Hvammstang.

"Come in," I called. The door opened and a friendly Danish face appeared.

"Excuse me. I was wondering why I haven't seen you up on deck. Are you sick?"

"No, I don't believe I am. I'll be up shortly."

Then the man bowed in a friendly fashion, closed the

door and went away. It was the captain. He was a nice man. All who don't demand money from paupers at sea are nice men.

That evening I sat at the captain's table with the boarding school girl. She had light gray eyes. My beloved was dark-eyed.

We were held up two days by fog and had to lie in port. No one had yet demanded that I pay my fare and I could unmolested watch my debt grow with each meal. On the evening of the second day I strolled about the deck. There was not a breath of wind and the moon occasionally peeked out from behind the clouds. My mood was a mixture of exalted love and a feeling that some miracle was soon about to take place, either that night or the next day.

The next morning the fog lifted and the sun came out and the sky was clear and blue. I crept up on deck as soon as I heard we were under way and waited to catch the first glimpse of my beloved's mountains. But what was this? We were headed straight west across the bay instead of south toward Hvammstang. What was wrong? Is my sight failing me? Or has the man gone crazy? I turned to one of the crew standing on the deck and shouted:

"What's happening? Aren't we going to Hvammstang?"
"No. We're going to Northfjord."
"Northfjord? What do you mean Northfjord?"
"We have cargo to leave there."
"But then we'll head back to Hvammstang."
"No, then we're going to Holmvik."
"Holmvik! But then to Hvammstang."
"No. We'll first stop at Hrutafjord before returning to Hvammstang."

"Are you crazy, man?"

He stared at me.

"In Akureyri they told me there would be only one stop before Hvammstang."

"They've changed the route."

"But this is outrageous!"

He walked away from me without answering.

Upon considering the situation closer I discovered that this change of route would be greatly to my advantage. I wouldn't be asked to pay before we came to Northfjord because they thought I was going to Hvammstang. That was the miracle. The greatest moments in life always come upon one unexpected. And they had now come upon me in such a way that I had no scruples about running off without paying my fare. I had been deceived and I would repay them in kind.

When we arrived at Northfjord I went down to the cabin, wrapped my shiny coat around my work shoes, laid it shrewdly over my left arm as if there were nothing in it, took my walking stick in my right hand, shut the door and went up on deck. By the bridge I met the captain. I greeted him cheerfully:

"I think I'll go ashore a minute. I have a little sister living here. And I want to buy some gloves. My hands are cold."

He answered like a kind father:

"Yes, do that. You haven't been ashore since we left Akureyri."

An accusing tone rang in my breast:

It's despicable to cheat such a nice man.

I attempted to quiet the voice of honesty and said to myself:

Well, it's not decided yet. Perhaps I won't do anything

but ask about the paths to Hrutafjord. And I'll probably leave it go at that.

Then my beloved appeared before my inner eye and I heard the rush of words she whispered in my ear:

"Oh, go ahead and cheat them. They deserve it. They're just a bunch of liars and swindlers."

She's undoubtedly right, I thought.

So I climbed down the ladder in almost shameless peace of mind, taking care not to let the work shoes fall out of the coat, and stepped into the dinghy that would take me ashore. It was as if a glacier had been lifted from my heart when I realized that this voyage was now a thing of the past.

Passing By

THIS RECKLESS expedition of mine had at least an auspicious start. As soon as I stepped ashore in Northfjord I ran into an extremely congenial old man who knew absolutely everything there was to know about the paths to Hrutafjord and who gave me all the information I needed. I pumped him for every scrap of information about distances, about each mountain, each heath, each fjord, each brook, directions, trails, cairns, farms and other places where I might stay. And when I had found out everything I needed to know I unhesitatingly determined to desert the ship and walk all the way to Borgarnes.

Naturally, it would have shortened my path considerably if I had taken the boat to Holmvik. But such a course had the distinct disadvantage that I might have been asked to pay my fare on the way, with resulting lawyers and a murky prison cell.

It would have been still less advisable to take the boat all the way to Hrutafjord, also with respect to another factor. It would then have been necessary for me to walk seven or eight miles back up Hrutafjord, in the exact opposite direction of Borgarnes, to meet my beloved. And such a detour could have awakened humorous comment and had an unfortunate influence upon our young and bashful love.

On the other hand, there would be nothing suspicious about my approaching from the north along the western shore of the fjord just like any other traveler. I could have been on any of a number of errands, and her farm would lie only a two or three minute walk off my path. And it is an ancient custom that travelers drop in at farms by the wayside for a drink of water. Who could then suspect that I coveted her innocence if I just dropped in, weary from my long journey over the mountains, and asked for a drink of water?

Taking everything into consideration, I could imagine no better opportunity to meet my beloved. It wasn't until years later, fortunately, that it occurred to me that the captain of the ship could have learned of my movements in Northfjord, telephoned to the sheriff in Hrutafjord to take me captive when I arrived there and turned me over to the lawyers and police in Reykjavik.

I obtained nourishing refreshments in Northfjord and brought a pair of mittens. I was asked why the devil I intended to hike all that long way when I could have just taken the boat? I said that I loved to see new country. It was almost four o'clock when I started off, apprehensive and lonely, like a fragile soul that is about to step over the threshold of a new existence.

I followed the southern shore of Northfjord. The ship lay so close to the shore that I could easily have been recognized by my new gray hat. So I took it off and folded it together and held it in the hand away from the ship until I was out of sight behind a slight rise. Occasionally I looked back. There was nothing suspicious in sight.

A good hour later I arrived at a farm. I was invited in and given coffee and cakes and a little white linen bag to put my good shoes in, along with a piece of cord so that I could carry the bag over my shoulder.

The sun had begun to set when I left the farm. The path led first over a small marsh, then up long green slopes that blushed in the diminishing light of the dying sun. Then through echoing ravines filled with the deepening shadows of the evening. Up on the mountain the view to the south was out over a glistening fjord that shimmered in the silvery rays of the full moon. That was Reykjafjord. The sun had set. The sky was clear and the stars sparkled brilliantly, it was breathlessly still and the fragrance of moss filled the air.

I was filled with a heavenly exultation that lifted my thoughts far above this wretched earth, this myopic world of jails and lawyers. Even my beloved was swept aside like a speck of dust in a blazing ray of light. At that moment all was foolishness and vanity except The Eternal. All worldly thoughts here became childishness. Weakness no longer asked about the purpose of life, nor fear about the grave and death. Love no longer inquired about the inclinations of the beloved, nor selfishness about gains and profits. There was only the limitless bliss of enlightened wisdom, of the eternal moment, of the everlasting now where everything *is*, nothing *was*, and nothing will become.

I worked my way down the side of the mountain to the fjord. And when I re-entered the mist-filled world of men the veil of worldly thoughts fell once more before my eyes.

The next day was cloudy, calm and quite warm. The path between Reykjafjord and Steingrimsfjord to the south was over a long and desolate heath covered with nothing but huge boulders. There was not so much as a withered blade of grass between the stones to break the monotony, not a spot of moss anywhere, nowhere the rippling of a brook, the bleating of a sheep, the twittering of a bird, only eternal death, only a grave-like silence as far as the eye could reach and the ear could hear.

When I finally came down off this heath I came to a peaceful little farm where I inquired about the path and asked for a drink of water. I was invited in and treated to coffee. I sat at the window and stared into the countenance of my beloved which I saw reflected in the fjord below the farm. I had come to Steingrimsfjord.

The next day, Tuesday the first of October, I continued my journey along the western and southern shore of Steingrimsfjord. During the afternoon the skies grew dark and it looked like rain. But the rain didn't come. Just before twilight I reached the top of a little ridge that separates Steingrimsfjord and Kollafjord. There were no paths and I found my way across the pass with the help of telephone poles. It was dark when I came to a farm where I could spend the night.

It was sometime between nine and ten the next morning when I left. I found my way up the mountainside along steep, tortuous paths and set out across the heath between Kollafjord and Bitrufjord. When I finally reached Bitrufjord I began once more to think about my beloved. Until then I had been hiking along in a state of intoxicated expectation of seeing her again. I felt that I had won a great victory over a despicable enemy each time the mountain ridges between us became fewer. Thus far I had put four such enemies behind me. Only one remained.

This was the first day that I could feel that strange exhilarating warmth which she always gave off to her surroundings. Never had she seemed to me so charming, so good and so noble. Never had her femininity been enveloped in so many enticing secrets. How she'll embrace me warmly when I finally stand before her! How she'll kiss me and speak beautiful words to me. Then I'll tell her: You're an innocent angel. I love you beyond the grave and death.

It was dusk when I finally reached the ridge above Hrutafjord and saw it lie stretched out at my feet in the grayish half-darkness. I started back. Was this her fjord? Did it really look like this? A little later I reached the next-to-last farm in Hrutafjord and stayed there that night. After supper I went to bed and sighed quietly: I wish this night would never end.

But the sun rose on another day, the most decisive day of the journey, the final goal of this long and strenuous pilgrimage.

On that unforgettable day I walked along the western shore of Hrutafjord. There was no way back now. I exerted myself to refrain from speculating about the coming meeting with my beloved. To keep my mind off her I sang stirring songs and recited strident ballads.

I tried to postpone the crucial moment as long as possible. I dropped in on a farmer I had met during the summer, practiced asking for a drink of water and was invited in for coffee. I sat there a long time.

Then I strolled along the path further, going slower and slower as I drew nearer to the blessed abode of my beloved. Well, well, there's the boat out in the fjord. This provided an unexpected opportunity to pause a while and recollect my sufferings aboard. What a lot of fun I had then! I traversed the last stages of the journey at a snail's pace. I crept slowly by Prestbakki and thought: Two farms left. Then past Ljotunnarstad. One farm left. I almost felt as if I were stumbling on trembling legs toward the bloody chopping-block. I was done for! Behind me shone sunny days, ahead lay pitch-dark night.

Finally further postponement was impossible. It was four-thirty. And not four-thirty in the morning. What do you think you're doing, dropping in to see me in broad daylight?! A fine name you'll get me. I'm no cheap little whore.

I stood suddenly at the crossroads from which a path led to her farm. It would take only two or three minutes to get there. There's the little slope where we sat together in the clear sunshine. The grass faded now. There's the little hollow full of smiling flowers. Now they're dead. And there are her windows, staring out at me like watching eyes weary of straining themselves to catch a glimpse of their beloved coming over the hill.

What should I do?

I stared a while down at the silent path as if I were awaiting an answer from some incontrovertible oracle hidden in the depths. Then a voice spoke to me through the silence: Insolent fool! Don't let yourself be seen standing there any longer. And something within me added: You'll undoubtedly meet her on one of the other farms farther down along the fjord, and when you meet her there you'll be another man. And almost without knowing what I was doing I turned once more along the road. I looked back over my shoulder only a very few times before the farm had disappeared for all time over the hill. Those watchful eyes had thus stared in vain during fifteen sorrowful weeks for a glimpse of their beloved.

I was walking along the same stretch of road where I had sung: My hope is kindled in the light of your eyes one sunny Sunday morning in June. How changed everything was now! The skies were overclouded and threatening. The silent, sad cloak of autumn covered the land. From nowhere came the smile of flowers, the song of birds, the fragrance of grass, and the radiant gleam of hope was extinguished.

Just at twilight I came to the second farm where my beloved might be. Just a couple of minutes off the road. I stopped a moment and looked at the house. Then the voice spoke to me through the silence again: Insolent fool! Don't let yourself be seen standing there any longer. And something within me added: She's probably in town or staying with her aunt. And you'll be another man this evening or tomorrow morning. Then I ran off, bearing the burden of two missed opportunities on my frail shoulders.

It was beginning to grow dark when I got to town. What a sight! The town had been transformed into a bloody battleground where innocent, defenseless lambs were being slaughtered wholesale. The square was covered with bleating tethered lambs and the quivering, bleeding bodies of lambs from which the heads had just been removed, many of them resembling the naked bodies of children. In the middle of this mayhem stood arrogant farmers with razor-sharp knives in their hands with which they slit throat after throat, spitting and cursing the while.

I shuddered at this horrible sight. Numb with disgust and desperation I wandered back and forth across the square with half-closed eyes until I finally stumbled upon an old man I had met earlier in the summer. He had stopped working and was already a bit tipsy. He greeted me jovially and took me to a shed on the edge of town. We sat on some old boards there and struck up a conversation in the darkness. He pulled a bottle out of his pocket and handed it to me. I gladly accepted the offer and took a good swallow.

"How many lambs have you slaughtered today, Jon?" I asked.

"Damned if I know. Maybe twenty or so."

"I've often wondered if they feel much when their throats are cut like that. What do you think?"

"They probably feel just as much as we would if a knife was stuck in our throats."

"Do you think it's that bad? My god, that must be awful! Don't you get tired of slaughtering all day?"

"Why should I get tired of it? It's just like any other work that God has given man. Where are you coming from, anyway? Weren't you headed for the herring fleet in Siglufjord this summer?"

"Yes, but when I got there there was no work to be had, so I went on to Akureyri. But tell me, Jon, is it common here in Hrutafjord that girls desert their sweethearts?"

"Oh, it's not exactly common, but it happens."

"They're not so loose around here then?"

"Well, they like it when they get it, the little bitches. But there haven't been so many illegitimate babies lately. Why do you ask about that?"

"Well, I'll tell you just exactly why. I'm a bit of a scientist and find it interesting to do research and compare conditions around the country with the way things are down south, where I was born and grew up. Not a single illegitimate baby was born down there in the sixteen years I lived at home. But it did happen once, on a nice spring day, that a girl who was walking between farms could see in the distance the possibility that she might acquire an illegitimate child. So she took to her heels and ran at top speed all the way to the nearest farm away from the possible father of her child whom she had seen far up on the mountainside. That's how pure the girls down south are."

"They're not so nimble around here, let me tell you."

"Aren't they really? Have there been any new engagements announced around here this summer?"

"Not that I know of."

"Have you heard about any new couples going around together?"

"Not that I can remember."

"Haven't the young people been taking riding trips together?"

"Oh, there's been a bit of stretching out here and there. But I really don't keep track of such things any longer."

"Isn't there a lot of wild drinking on these trips?"

"Not so much the last few years."

"Is everyone in good health around here?"

"Oh, I suppose so."

"No one's been seriously ill?"

"I don't think so."

"And no one's died?"

"Not that I've heard."

"And everyone's still working away on the same old farms?"

"People don't go moving around right in the middle of the harvest."

"No, of course not. I just meant if extra hands had left one farm to work at another."

"Not that I remember."

"I suppose there are a lot of people who will be leaving for school in Reykjavik soon."

"Oh, there's always some."

"You haven't perhaps heard about anyone who's decided not to go back to school?"

"No, not that I've heard about."

I had begun to see that there was no sense in continuing this horrible conversation. I had exhausted all possible approaches and didn't have the courage to go right to the heart of the matter. I stood up, shook Jon's hand and thanked him for everything. Then I fumbled my way out of the shed and went to the hotel. I slept there that night.

The next day it was still cloudy and calm, but it was easy to see that a change was about to come. The clouds were heavier and the air more laden with rain. I slept late in order to avoid letting people see such a miserable fool as I was in broad daylight. About two o'clock I paid my hotel bill and sneaked out of town unnoticed.

I walked slowly along the shore of the fjord and the echoing of memories in my mind brought back to life one event after the other. We had ridden along these very paths together the evening I left Hrutafjord. The sky was dark and threatening then, too. Just here on this little hill she turned her rosy cheeks toward me and her full lips parted as if she were going to laugh at something. And I said to myself: What is she going to laugh at? But then she didn't laugh. Just there at the bend of the stream she glanced to both sides like a traveler looking for a soft bed of grass to sit on. There in the hollow she sent me a puzzling glance. And she looked tired and there was hopelessness in her eyes. As we let our horses struggle up this slope I had intended to present her with all my views on

God and love. And across that stretch of sand she had galloped her horse and her body had rocked rhythmically and lushly in the saddle.

After I had been walking about a half hour I came to the last farm where I could imagine my beloved might possibly be. The road ran right past the house. But I didn't stop. I didn't ask for a drink of water. I just hurried past and continued on my way. And when my body and soul had returned to equilibrium after this last great effort to save the reputation of both of us I said calmly to myself: It doesn't make any difference. We'll meet in Reykjavik in two weeks.

Oblivion

As I TURNED into High Street I caught sight of a man squatting on a large stone near the corner. He was staring into the darkness and seemed to be sunk in solemn thoughts.

"Good evening, Tryggvi," I said.

"Good evening," he answered. "Oh, is it you? When did you arrive?"

"Just now. I was hoping to see you soon to ask you if I could pick up the two bags you brought for me from Akureyri."

"One of them is in my room, but I'm sorry about the other. I asked a sailor I knew to keep an eye on it, but now he denies ever having seen it. I'm afraid he's stolen it."

"Which bag do you have?"

"The poorer one. He stole the large one."

"And everything that was in it?"

"Yes, and everything that was in it."

"Oh, well, I guess it doesn't make much difference. But what are you doing sitting on a stone in the darkness?"

"I'm tired of life."

"Tired of life!"

"Yes, I long for oblivion."

"Why the hell do you long for oblivion?"

"Things are going bad. I can't forget Catherine Nordmann. What'll I do?"

"Is there an organ in the house you live in?"

"Yes, there's one downstairs."

"Are you allowed to play on it?"

"Whenever I want."

"Well, then you should advertise yourself as an organ teacher and the girls will come running. And then stroke their necks."

"Stroke their necks? Does that soften them up?"

"I have been told that any woman can be won over by stroking her neck."

My friend sank still deeper in thought.

"Well, Tryggvi," I continued, "think it over. But now I've got to get home and get something to eat. I haven't eaten anything since 7:30 this morning. I'll pick up my bag tomorrow evening and then we can discuss your future at greater length."

So I bid my friend and benefactor farewell and headed for No. 10 High Street.

Finis

THE NEXT MORNING I sat at my work table in my room and began copying The Ballad of Reading Gaol by Oscar Wilde, a long poem of 108 verses about human suffering which I intended to show to my beloved when she came to town.

And the longer I compared my thoughts about the death of true love with my memory of two soft, white hands that had long before lain on this plain, crude table, the clearer my constant heart understood that it was beyond the power of my hands ever to stroke any other girl's neck.

Saturday the twenty-sixth of this month the *Western Seas* arrives from Borgarnes.